The LIGHT WITCH
D0273907

To Sheena, with love

ORCHARD BOOKS
96 Leonard Street, London EC2A 4XD
Orchard Books Australia
32/45-51 Huntley Street, Alexandria, NSW 2015
ISBN 1-84362-189-4
First published in Great Britain in 2004
A paperback original

A CIP catalogue record for this book is available from the British Library.
1 3 5 7 9 10 8 6 4 2
Printed in Great Britain

The LIGHT WITCH

Book 3: The Time of the Stars

Andrew Matthews

ORCHARD BOOKS

Titles in *the Light Witch* Trilogy:

Shadowmaster
The Darkening
The Time of the Stars

Prologue: A Dirty Snowball

Joe Farmer put his head around the lounge door. 'Come on, Jack,' he said to his son. 'I've got something to show you.'

'What?' said Jack, not shifting his eyes from the TV.

'It's a surprise.'

Jack groaned inwardly. He knew about his father's surprises. Dad had once woken him at six in the morning and dragged him all the way down the back garden, just because some manky robin had built a nest in the privet hedge.

Jack pulled a face and said, 'But the football starts in five minutes.'

'Never mind football! This is a once-in-a-lifetime opportunity.'

Jack did some rapid calculation. Normally he would have told his father to get lost, and settled down to watch the game, but his fourteenth birthday was coming up. He was hoping to touch Dad for an increase in his allowance, and he'd stand a better chance of success if he kept his old man sweet. With a put-upon sigh, Jack zapped off the TV and hauled himself on to his feet.

'We going far?' he asked.

'Aha!' said Joe, tapping the side of his nose. 'That's for me to know and you to find out, innit?'

The drive through town was quiet. There was hardly any traffic around, mainly, Jack reflected bitterly, because most sensible people were watching the match. He clocked the binoculars on the back seat and said, 'Where you taking me?'

'Up the Speaking Stones.'

'Da-ad!' Jack snorted. 'I've seen 'em loads of times! What's the big deal about looking at a bunch of old stones stuck in a field?'

'We're not going to look at the stones. There's something else I want you to see.'

'What – grass? Oh, super!'

'Less of your lip, laddie!' Joe snarled. 'You've been getting a bit too big for your boots lately.'

Joe only said it because his father used to say it to him, but he didn't add what his dad had always added

– a clip round the ear – though there were times when he was tempted. Jack was deep in his sullen, mouthy teen phase, and waiting for him to grow out of it put a strain on Joe's patience. It might have been easier if he'd been able to share the strain with Angela, but they'd broken up when Jack was seven.

No point dwelling on the past, Joe said to himself – another saying he'd got from his father.

Joe parked on the top of Stanstowe Hill, and he and Jack got out. Joe rescued the binoculars, locked the car and led the way into the centre of an ancient stone circle. Sunset was over and dusk was creeping in, softening the edges of the stones with powdery shadows. Down below in Stanstowe, the street lamps were coming on, glowing pink before stuttering into orange. Overhead, the sky was a greenish grey.

'Look,' said Joe, pointing upwards.

Jack looked and saw tiny points of brightness.

'You brought me up here to look at *stars*?' he said, his voice breaking in a squeak.

'They're not stars, they're planets,' said Joe. 'More planets together than you'll see in a long time. The big one's Jupiter, and the pale one to the right of it is Saturn. Mars is the yellowy job over there, and the one right down low is Venus. Four planets for the price of one. Not bad, eh?'

'Hmm!' said Jack, wondering if the team he supported had scored yet.

'But that's not all, Jack. See that long streak under Jupiter? What d'you reckon that is?'

'Vapour trail.'

Joe chuckled.

'Now that's where you're wrong,' he said. 'That streak, my son, is Comet Bailey-Hooper. Last time anyone saw it in the sky was six thousand years ago, and it won't be back for another six thousand.'

Joe handed Jack the binoculars and Jack tried to find the streak. It was difficult because the throbbing of his pulse made his hands shake, but at last he got the comet in the binoculars' field of vision. It looked like a long, straggly feather.

'You know, back in the old days they thought comets were harbingers of doom that brought war and plagues and that,' said Joe. 'Actually, they're just big, dirty snowballs.'

'Is that right?' said Jack, pretending to be interested.

Then he heard a sound that wasn't so much a note

as a pressure in his eardrums that grew until it became painful.

Jack lowered the binoculars to glance at his father, and noticed that the Speaking Stones seemed to be moving, rippling as though they'd been turned to jelly.

'Here, Dad?' Jack murmured.

'What?'

'What's happening to the stones?'

His ears popped and cracked, and the stones were solid again.

Joe looked around. 'Nothing's happening to the stones,' he said. 'You can't concentrate on anything for more than five minutes, can you? You ought to remember that comet. It'll be something you'll be able to tell your own kids about.'

'Yeah,' said Jack. 'Dad, can we go now? I'm getting cold.'

Joe frowned. The air was as heavy and sticky as sweat.

'What d'you mean, cold?' he said. 'It's got to be at least fifteen degrees and— Oh, I get it. Football, eh? One day you'll learn that there's more to life than football.'

But it wasn't football, and Jack was relieved when

his father turned and walked back towards the car. He could feel something in the darkness gathering around the stones, something that he wanted to get away from.

1
Hot Spell

Dido had PE last lesson. When the final bell rang, she and Philippa left the changing rooms and went to sit on the bench near the main gate, to wait for Scott and Ollie. It was part of a long-established routine: Philippa and Ollie lived near each other and walked part of the way home together; Dido and Scott caught the same bus.

Philippa flopped on to the bench, wrinkled up her nose and declared, 'This isn't right!'

'What isn't?' said Dido.

'This.' Philippa flapped her hand to indicate the entire school. 'It's the end of term next week. End of term should be fizzy, kind of *boing*! and *whee*! This is more, *splud*!'

'It's too hot to do anything but splud.'

Dido wasn't in the best of moods. Despite the shower she'd just taken, she was already hot and sticky again and she knew that her face was beetroot-coloured. Philippa, on the other hand, looked great, even though she was wearing a battered baseball cap and had white smears of sunblock on her nose and lips.

'And that's something else that's not right,' Philippa said. 'Last Easter it rained almost every day. It's too early in the year to be this hot.'

Philippa wasn't the only one who thought so. The end of the day at Prince Arthur Comp was generally a loud, chaotic tidal wave, but today the trickle of pupils leaving the school was uncharacteristically quiet. No one goofed, ran or shouted. People with open collars and rolled-up sleeves slouched through the shimmering air.

'Everybody's so ratty,' Philippa grumbled. 'Like, all winter they moan about the cold and bang on about how they can't wait for the summer, but as soon as there's a heatwave, they complain about that as well. Can't you do something about it?'

'What?'

'The weather.' Philippa leaned in closer and spoke quietly. 'Isn't there a spell you could cast that would—'

'Sorry,' said Dido. 'If there *are* spells powerful

enough to change the weather, they're way out of my league.'

'Oh,' said Philippa, sounding disappointed. 'Couldn't you conjure us up an ice cream or something?'

'No need,' Dido said. 'There's an ice-cream van just down the road.'

Philippa laughed.

'Tell me, Dido,' she said, 'does being a witch *ever* come in handy?'

'Yes, at the right time and place,' said Dido.

Philippa wasn't joking, Dido actually *was* a witch, and her parents were witches too. They practised Light Magic, a magic used to help other people. Originally, all magic had been Twilight Magic, until the evil Lord Spelkor had divided it into Light and Shadow. Spelkor's followers were called Shadowmasters, and used their powers to cause pain and misery. Light Witches followed the Goddess.

Philippa put on her girls-together voice and said, 'There's one good thing about the hot weather though – Scott's tan. It suits him.'

'Does it?'

Philippa's eyes widened.

'Haven't you noticed?' she said. 'It really brings out

his teeth and his eyes. Scott has great teeth and eyes, doesn't he?'

'Sure,' said Dido. 'He can see and eat like anything.'

'You know what I mean!'

'Yes I do, and I'm not the one you should be saying it to. Why don't you ask Scott out on a date and get it over with?'

Philippa sighed.

'It's not that easy,' she said. 'He has to ask me, because then I'll know that he likes me. If I ask him and he says no, it might make things awkward, you know? It might spoil our friendship.'

'Well if the friendship's that important to you, forget about fancying him,' said Dido.

'I can't help it!' Philippa wailed. 'I didn't know that Scott would suddenly turn into a hunk at the beginning of term, but now that he has, I can't stop thinking about him. You don't understand what it's like, Dido.'

As a matter of fact, Philippa was dead wrong. Dido understood only too well, and as if to emphasise her understanding, Ollie and Scott appeared around the corner of C Block. The afternoon sun burned in Ollie's red hair as he smiled and waved.

As always, Ollie's smile sent Dido's stomach on a roller-coaster ride, a sensation she'd never quite been able to get used to. Unfortunately, she suspected that the smile was more for Philippa's benefit than hers.

Scott didn't smile. He gangled along, his head held low and his shoulders slumped, self-conscious about his height. He'd been a bit of a runt in Year Seven, a chatterbox and a klutz who cracked corny jokes, did clumsy conjuring tricks and had dreams of being an escape artist when he grew up. All that had changed by Year Nine. Scott had turned into a moody teenager, and there were days when he was decidedly prickly. By the look on his face, it was one of those days. His eyes were fixed on the ground and his mouth was pulled down at the corners.

The four friends chatted for a few minutes – or rather, Dido, Philippa and Ollie chatted while Scott hung like a rain cloud in the background – and then split into pairs to go their separate ways.

When she was alone with Scott, the only thing that Dido could think of to say was, 'Isn't it hot today?'

'Mmm,' said Scott.

'Doing anything tonight?'

'Homework. TV.'

Starting a conversation with Scott was like extracting wisdom teeth. Dido had hoped to get around to the subject gradually, but the subtle approach obviously wasn't going to work, so she said, 'Scott, have you ever considered – I mean, would you ever—?'

'Would I ever what?'

Dido took a deep breath.

'Ask Philippa out,' she said.

Scott was so startled that he looked up and made eye contact.

'Huh?' he said.

'Ask Philippa out,' Dido said again.

'Why?'

'Because she wants you to.'

Scott shook his head.

'No, she wants *someone* to ask her out,' he said. 'She figures it's time that she had a boyfriend, and because I'm around, I'll do. Thanks, but no thanks.'

'She's really pretty,' Dido pointed out.

'I know.'

'She likes you a lot.'

Angry sparks glowed in Scott's eyes.

'Get off my case, will you, Dido?' he snapped. 'The only reason you want me and Philippa to be an item is because it'll give you a clear shot at Ollie. You've been making puppy eyes at him for months.'

'No I haven't!' protested Dido, but she had, and she was shocked that Scott had noticed. 'Ollie understands magic because he has second sight, so I can talk to him about witch stuff. He's just a friend.'

'Yeah, that's your problem, isn't it?'

Dido quickly hid behind a protection spell. The magic tingled against her skin, producing the same goose-pimple sensation as stepping into a hot bath. Nothing showed on the outside, but inside a coat of chain mail wove itself from ice until Dido's feelings were completely armoured.

'And what's *your* problem?' she demanded coldly.

Scott went very still for a second and stared straight at Dido, then he melted into a shrug and lowered his head.

'What's the point?' he said. 'You wouldn't believe me if I told you.'

He increased his pace and walked on ahead.

Dido was dismayed. Scott had never avoided her before, and it left her with a feeling that she didn't like.

Being a witch has always been a hassle, she thought, but being a teen *really* sucks!

And there was more to being a witch than just a hassle. Dido's last birthday, her thirteenth, had been her Covening, and she'd come of age as a witch. Since then her magical powers had grown, as she'd expected they would. What she hadn't been expecting was that her magic would develop a mind of its own. Some spells came to her without warning, and when that happened she didn't quite know what to do. It was as if there were times when magic was in control of her, instead of the other way round.

What with one thing and another, getting older wasn't any fun at all.

When Dido got home, she found her father working in the back garden. Dad had moved the garden table and chairs on to the patio, into the shade of a big rowan tree. Dressed in a baggy T-shirt, shorts and flip-flops, he was clacking away at a laptop, pausing every now and then to wipe sweat from his forehead.

Dido loaded two tall glasses with ice from the freezer, poured in fizzy mineral water and carried them outside. She held out one of the glasses and said, 'There you go. You look like you need cooling down.'

Dad took the glass with a grateful smile.

'Have I ever told you that you're the most wonderful daughter in the world?' he said.

'Not recently.' Dido pulled out a chair and sat down. 'What are you writing?'

'A review of a voice-activation system for laptops. You speak to the computer, and it does what you tell it.'

'Any good?'

'If it was, I'd be dictating the review instead of typing it.'

'You should have used magic to get it to work,' Dido said.

'Somehow I don't think so. Putting "if all else fails, try a persuasion spell" in the instruction manual wouldn't go down well.'

The shrubbery twitched and a large black she-cat with yellowy-orange eyes emerged on to the patio, purring loudly. The cat's age showed in her round stomach and the slight stiffness of her movements, but her coat was thick and glossy.

'Hi, Cosmo,' said Dido. 'It's good to see you too.'

Cosmo trilled.

'Not so bad,' said Dido. 'Same old, same old.'

'Excuse me?' said Dad.

'I was talking to Cosmo,' Dido explained. 'She

asked me how school was today.'

Dad took a thoughtful sip of iced water.

'Can you really understand what Cosmo says, or is it a wind-up?' he asked.

'No wind-up. Cosmo and I have a special relationship.'

'But she's the family's familiar!' said Dad. 'Spirit guides shouldn't have favourites.'

'Try telling her that.'

Dad suddenly grimaced, put the tip of a little finger into his right ear and wiggled it.

'There's that damned voice again!' he snarled. 'It's been driving me mad all day. Someone must have their windows open and their radio on just loud enough for it to be distracting.'

Dido listened. There wasn't a sound in the garden, not even the rustling of a breeze in the leaves of the rowan.

'I don't hear anything,' she said.

'It comes and goes,' said Dad. 'I tried a blocking spell, but it didn't take.'

'Dad,' Dido said, 'if you like someone, but you're not sure how much they like you, should you tell them or keep quiet? Because if they don't like you as much as you like them, and they tell you after you tell them, you'll know, but if you don't, you won't, will you?'

Dad scratched his chin.

'Let's do a deal, Dido,' he said. 'You teach me how to speak Cat, and I'll teach you how to speak English, OK?'

2
Warning

Say something, you jerk! thought Ollie. Tell her before you get to the next corner. Don't leave it another day!

He cleared his throat and said, 'Er, Philippa?'

Philippa turned her head to look at him, and as she did, Ollie had an unexpected rush of second sight.

The aura of energy that surrounded Philippa was pale blue, but shot through with streaks of dark silver, a sure sign of inner turmoil. Within the aura, Philippa's face flipped backwards and forwards through time, showing Ollie what she'd looked like as a child, then what she'd look like as an adult and an old woman. All the faces made him ache as he realised that he'd love Philippa no matter what age she was.

'What?' said Philippa.

Ollie's nerve failed.

'Anything up?' he said. 'You're a bit quiet.'

'It's the heat.'

Ollie knew that she wasn't telling the truth. Philippa's aura had shown him that she was depressed about something that ought to be making her happy, and he found the mix of emotions as confusing as she did.

'Only, if something's up, you can always talk to me about it,' he said.

Philippa smiled in a way that raised Ollie's hopes.

'I know,' she said. 'I'm always bending your ear. I couldn't have got through all that stuff when Dad married Alison last year, if it hadn't been for you.'

Ollie thought, Now! Say it! It's easy. I I—, but he couldn't get the words out. Instead, he said, 'Are things still all right?'

'Alison and I are doing fine. We get ratty with each other sometimes, but I don't hate her any more. I can't remember why I ever did.'

Ollie felt defeated. The right moment had fallen away like a stone dropping down a well.

'I can't stand hot sunny weather,' he said, changing the subject. 'It brings me out in freckles that make me look about nine years old.'

'I like freckles,' said Philippa. 'They're kind of cute.'

There it was again, a chance for Ollie to open up and offload the heavy weight in the pit of his stomach.

'Scott was in a humpty mood today,' said Philippa. 'What's his story?'

'Oh, you know how sulky guys can get when the hormones hit their bloodstream,' Ollie said evasively. He knew exactly what Scott's story was – Scott was in love with Dido – but Ollie discovered it via second sight, and it would be like betraying Scott if he told Philippa.

'*You* don't get sulky,' Philippa said.

'No, I get romantic.'

Philippa raised her eyebrows.

'You do?' she said. 'Anyone in particular?'

Ollie was teetering on the brink of a chasm, and if he leaned forward he'd either fly or plummet.

'Um, four people actually,' he said. 'You know that girl band, Jagged Mink? Them.'

Philippa cracked up.

'You're kidding!' she giggled.

'I've got a poster of them on my bedroom wall.'

'But Jagged Mink make music for Junior school kids!'

'I don't listen to their music,' Ollie said. 'When they're on TV, I turn down the sound and just watch.'

'You perv!'

'Hey, I'm a guy who fancies girls – what's pervy about that?'

A far-off look came into Philippa's eyes.

'You know, I've always thought what a great couple you and Dido would make,' she said. 'You've got a lot in common.'

The world collapsed on top of Ollie.

'Yeah,' he said. 'We're both weird.'

Philippa didn't disagree, and the world collapsed again.

When they reached the street where Philippa lived, she said goodbye and walked away. Ollie watched her until she reached the driveway of her house, his eyes unwilling to let her go. She didn't turn to look back at him.

Why would she? Ollie thought miserably. I'm an ear that she bends, that's all.

He made for home, thinking how everything was a mess, and that he was the only one who knew precisely how big a mess.

He could imagine it chalked in four hearts on a playground wall.

If he hadn't been one of the names involved, Ollie might have thought that it was funny.

For most of the rest of the way home, Ollie tortured himself with daydreams about himself and Philippa holding hands at the movies, or sharing the same umbrella in the rain, or strolling along a tropical beach at sunset. The fact that the daydreams were terminally corny and naff didn't make them any less painful.

Then, on Alder Drive, Ollie ran into some serious weirdness. The first thing he noticed was the drop in temperature and the dimming of the sunshine. There was a smell that tasted as bitter as paracetamol. A fine dust sifted through the air, and Ollie couldn't help inhaling some of it.

Alder Drive looked terrible. All the houses, trees,

parked cars and pedestrians were coated with dust, a thin layer of purple-grey grime. Ollie could feel it settling on his hair and skin. His eyes streamed and he sneezed violently. Looking up from the sneeze, he saw the top of Stanstowe Hill over the roofs of the houses. The hill appeared to be on fire, sending a tall column of dark smoke into the sky.

Ollie heard a faint whisper, a scratchy sound, like the buzzing of an insect trapped in a jar. He concentrated, trying to make out the words ...

The street brightened. The dust, smell, whispering, and the smoke on Stanstowe Hill vanished.

Ollie frowned. His second sight had given him a vision of something that was happening, or was going to happen. The vision was obviously intended as a warning, but a warning about what?

A couple of months ago, Ollie wouldn't have hesitated to contact Dido and arrange a meeting to talk the vision over with her, but now he wasn't so sure that it was a good idea. When he and Dido were together, he knew that she was eating her heart out over him, the same way that he ate his heart out when he was with Philippa.

Maybe the vision was straightforward. Maybe

some kids were going to start a fire in the dry grass on Stanstowe Hill. It was nice of his second sight to give him a sneak preview, but Ollie decided that dealing with it was a job best left to the fire brigade.

Dido's mother didn't come in until gone six. Dido and Dad were in the kitchen, chopping vegetables and soaking rice. Mum leaned against the frame of the kitchen door and suppressed a yawn.

'You're late,' said Dad.

'It's Wednesday,' Mum said. 'Wednesdays is when I give Alice her after-school lesson.'

Mum was a deputy head at Prince Arthur's. Alice – Miss Morgan to Dido – was a Drama teacher at the school, and also an untrained witch. A year ago, Dido had rescued Miss Morgan from the evil influences of Shadow Magic, which had tried to take her over. Now, with help from Mum, Miss Morgan was learning Light Magic.

'How's she getting along?' Dido asked.

Mum rolled her eyes.

'Today's session was a wash-out,' she said. 'Neither of us could get anything right. We managed to break a wastepaper bin.'

'How can you break a wastepaper bin?'

'By having a lifting spell go wrong,' said Mum. 'Instead of lifting the bin, the spell tore it in half. My magic seems to be all over the place at the moment.'

'Mine too,' said Dido. 'Dad, are you crying?'

'It's the onions,' said Dad. He turned to Mum. 'You should have invited Alice over for a meal and done the lesson here. It would have relaxed you both.'

'And have you drooling over her all evening?' Mum said.

'I don't drool over her!'

'True,' Mum agreed, 'but you are over attentive. "Can I get you anything, Alice? Would you like a cushion, Alice?"'

'That's being hospitable,' said Dad, pretending to be offended. 'There's nothing leery about it. Good grief, I'm old enough to be Alice's uncle.'

Mum laughed, winced and raised a hand to her forehead.

'Headache?' said Dido.

'More like heatstroke. My office was so stuffy today. I wish the school could afford to install air-conditioning.'

'How about an electric fan?' Dad suggested.

'We can't afford those either.'

Dido recalled her conversation with Philippa, and

said, ‘Could we use magic to cool the place down?’

‘Not Light Magic,’ Mum said. ‘Mucking about with Mother Nature is a definite no-no.’

‘Can Shadow Magic change the weather?’

There was a moment of deathly hush before Dad said, ‘You’re the expert on Shadowmasters, Dido. You tell us.’

The way he said it made Dido regret that she’d mentioned anything about Shadow Magic, and reminded her of a whole bunch of stuff that she’d sooner forget.

Fate, she thought. There’s no escaping it, but you don’t know where it’s taking you until you get there.

Magic couldn’t alter anyone’s fate; if it could, Dido would already have used it to alter hers. In fact there were times when she would gladly have swapped her magical powers for a safe, normal life, with no complications.

3
Encounters

Scott walked in on a row. He could hear his sisters' raised voices before he opened the front door.

'Great!' he muttered. 'Guess who's going to have to sort it out?'

Normally when his sisters disagreed – which was only all the time – Scott could depend on the support of his kid brother Chris. Unfortunately, Chris was on a school trip to France and wouldn't be back until after Easter, so Scott was on his own. The house felt crowded at the best of times, but whenever there was any kind of tension in Scott's family, the walls closed in and squeezed. One of these days everyone was going to argue with everyone else and the roof would pop off.

Kate and Julie were red-facing each other in the hall. Their row was at the 'Did! Didn't!' stage.

'What's going on?' Scott said.

Julie held up a sheet of paper that had once been a painting but was now a soggy, blurred mess. There were the mucky tracks of dried tears on Julie's cheeks and she was so upset that she hiccuped when she spoke.

'I did this in school,' she said. 'Miss Tennant gave me a gold star for it, and I brought it home to show Mum, and Kate went and chucked water over it, and I hate her!'

'I did not chuck water over it!' yelled Kate. 'I was drinking a glass of water and you ran into me. Mum's told you hundreds of times not to run in the house. It was an accident, and it was your fault.'

'Was not!'

'Was!'

'Was not!'

'OK, OK!' said Scott. 'Tell you what, Jools, why don't you do another picture for Mum? I'll let you use my drawing pad and paints.'

'In your room?' Julie said slyly. Scott's room was forbidden territory, a part of the house that Julie didn't know as well as the rest. She liked the grown-up feel of it when she went in there, though Scott usually threw a pillow at her if she dared to.

'All right, in my room,' Scott said.

Tears forgotten, Julie thundered up the stairs.

'You shouldn't have done that, Scott,' Kate said sullenly. 'It's like rewarding her for being naughty. The little brat's always getting her own way.'

'Give her a break, will you, Kate! She's only six.'

'Yeah? Well I'm sixteen. I've got my GCSEs coming up in the summer, but do I get any consideration from anybody? Fat chance! If it's not the brat charging around like a rogue elephant, it's you playing that Thrash-Metal crap at full blast. Hasn't anyone ever told you about headphones?'

Another row was threatening, hanging in the air like static electricity looking for somewhere to earth itself.

Scott had plenty of ammunition to come back at Kate: the hours she spent on the phone and in the bathroom, the smooching she did right under Scott's bedroom window when the zitty gorilla she was going out with walked her home from a date.

Scott was loaded up and ready to let rip, but his irritation suddenly went flat. The row was bound to go like all his rows with Kate, round in circles. He untied his school jumper from around his waist, hung it over the newel post, stepped over to the hallstand and slipped on the well-worn leather jacket his brother Matt had handed down to him before leaving for university.

'What are you doing?' said Kate.

'Going out.'

'Wearing that? You'll boil.'

'And like you'd care?' said Scott.

He let the front door slam behind him.

Outside in the street, depression set in.

You really screwed up with Dido today, didn't you? a voice said in Scott's mind. She's the best mate you've ever had, but that's not good enough for you, is it? Oh no! You've got to go and get a massive crush on her, haven't you? After what you said about her and Ollie, she probably won't speak to you again. Face it, Scott, the only thing you're good at is being a loser.

The voice was Dad's. It had been almost four years since Scott's father had walked out, but if Scott did anything wrong, he heard his father in his head, having a go at him.

Scott blanked everything out, the voice, the heat and the hurt, and just walked.

He ended up in Hunter Park, near the adventure playground where his dad used to badger him to climb higher, swing longer, run faster. Skirting the playground and nearby tennis courts, Scott passed the statue of Ezra Hunter, the biscuit tycoon who'd been MP for Stanstowe in the 1860s. The statue was cast in bronze, and showed Ezra gazing out in stern Victorian disapproval as he clutched at a folded umbrella.

He should have posed with the umbrella open over his head, thought Scott. It would have protected him from the pigeons.

He followed the path that ran around the outside of the park. If he timed it right, Mum would be home from work when he got back. She'd sort Kate and Jools out, and Scott could get on with his homework in peace.

Someone called out, 'Well, well, well! Look who it isn't.'

Scott half-turned and saw Jack Farmer, Ross Williams and David Miller. They were in the same form as Scott, Dido and Philippa, and were known by the rest of the form – and the rest of Prince Arthur's – as the 'Terrible Trio'. The three boys were lolling on a bench, with cigarettes and cans of lager in their hands. Scott guessed that the lager had come via Ross, who looked way older than fourteen. He had the build and facial hair of a fully mature werewolf.

'Fancy a swig?' said Jack, offering Scott his can.

'I don't drink,' said Scott.

'Fag?'

'I don't smoke.'

Jack curled his top lip into a sneer.

'Don't drink, don't smoke, don't go out with girls!' he scoffed. 'What do you do, Scott, stay in and make your own dresses?'

Ross and David tittered.

Scott controlled a surge of irritation and said, 'Great sense of humour, guys, but then you'd need it to hang out with one another.'

Jack smiled.

'You still knock about with that Dido Nesbit, don't you?' he said. 'Turned into a bit of a babe, that one. She up for it?'

Something inside Scott fractured, and rage erupted inside him. He stepped over to the bench, grabbed Jack by the shoulders and yanked him upright. Jack's can fell to the path in a shower of lager.

'You say anything like that about Dido again,' said Scott, 'and I'll—'

Jack's features seemed to melt. They shifted and altered shape, and suddenly Scott was staring into his father's face.

Scott had never been so angry. It was as if he'd tapped into an outer source of fury that was using him as a pipeline. He wanted to smash the face in front of him. He couldn't tell if it was Jack's or Dad's any more, and he didn't care.

Strong hands seized him and pulled him back. He stumbled and fell, striking his elbow on the path. The sharp pain jolted him back to reality. Ross loomed above him, big enough and stupid enough to be dangerous.

Jack said, 'Leave it, Ross! He's not worth it. I can't stick people who can't take a joke.'

Ross looked Scott straight in the eyes and said, 'You mess with Jack, you mess with me, right?'

Scott said, 'Right,' because he knew that if he didn't, Ross would make him.

How did I get here? Scott thought. What got into me?

He was afraid of Ross, but he was more afraid of himself.

John Loomis' day had been a bummer from beginning to end. It started with him being late for work, for which he got grief from the store manager. Then he'd cut some lengths of wood the wrong size, and the customer had called over the manager to give John a second rollicking. At lunchtime, his can of fizzy drink had fizzed all over his overalls, which meant that the cost of cleaning them would be deducted from his pay. John reckoned that three bits of bad luck in a row was his lot for the day, but he reckoned wrong.

The cherry on the top of the cupcake was being stood up. John had chatted up a girl in a club on Saturday night. He was certain that she'd given him the come-on, and she'd agreed to meet him at the multiplex cinema on Wednesday night. Only she didn't show. Maybe she'd been too drunk on Saturday to remember.

So that was it – Wednesday night, money in his pocket and no one to spend it on but himself. He could go to the pub where his mates hung out, but the snag was he'd boasted to them about the girl, and if he showed his face this early, they'd suss that he'd been stood up and give him loads of stick, which he didn't need right now. Besides, he was feeling restless. He needed to get out of town, go somewhere that was in the open, breathe fresh air instead of exhaust fumes.

John wasn't much given to whims, but at that

moment one occurred to him, and his face stretched into a grin.

'The Speaking Stones,' he said to himself. 'Haven't been up there in ages.'

John picked up his scooter from where he'd left it in the cinema car park, strapped on his helmet and set off.

Getting to the Speaking Stones was great. John gave the throttle plenty of welly, and the wind rushing over him cooled him down a treat. Once he arrived at the circle though, he was puzzled. Why had he wanted to come? It was nearly dark, and there wasn't that much to look at. Apart from the stones and the view over Stanstowe, the place he was trying to escape from, the only thing of interest was the comet all the papers were banging on about, the one that was going to come within a few million kilometres of Earth. 'A Near Miss' the press called it, like millions of kilometres was across the street or something.

Still, thought John, since I'm here, I may as well stroll around for old times' sake.

This turned out to be not such a good idea, because as he entered the circle, fragments of old times returned to him, flashing disjointed pictures and sounds into his mind – faces, firelight, chanting, the terrified squeaking of a small animal. John had locked them all away, but now the lid of the box was wide open and all kinds of stuff came crawling out.

Did we really do that? John thought. Did we really say those things? Nah! We couldn't have. We were just a couple of kids fooling around.

And then, as if to prove him wrong, a dark figure stepped out from behind the circle's tallest stone and said, 'Hello, Johnno. Been a long time, hasn't it?'

John's pulse went like a champion greyhound. He leaned forward, squinting.

'Bivco?' he said uncertainly.

'The very same.'

Bivco came close. Impossibly, he looked the same as he had three years before when he was fifteen, only bigger.

'Bivco!' John said. 'When did you—?'

'Six months ago,' said Bivco, smiling his lopsided, crooked-toothed smile. 'Been in London for a while.'

'How are you, mate?'

'Like I spent the last three years in a school for young offenders, Johnno, how d'you think?'

'Sorry, I didn't mean—'

'Doesn't matter, Johnno. Remember when we did that?'

Bivco pointed at a stone to his right. John could just about make out that it had been written on with a spray can. **Bivco & Loomis** – Billy Cooper and John Loomis.

'Did it together, Johnno,' said Bivco. 'We did everything together, didn't we?'

'That's right, Biv.'

Bivco threw his arm around John's shoulders.

'And now I'm back,' he said. 'Back in Stanstowe and back in business. I've heard the call, Johnno.'

'What call's that then, Biv?'

Bivco winked.

'If you listen carefully enough, you'll hear it too,' he said. 'The stones never forget, Johnno.'

Bivco had a strange gleam in his eyes. The gleam was strange because, from where he was standing, John could have sworn that it was purple.

4
Getting Ready

It was cold in Dido's dream. Wintery drizzle fell from a dark grey sky. She hurried through the centre of Stanstowe, heading towards the railway station. No traffic passed along the roads and the pavements were empty.

Dido climbed the steps near the bay where the Heathrow coaches parked, and entered the station concourse. Ollie was waiting for her, seated at one of the aluminium tables outside a coffee bar. He didn't smile when he saw her. His face was pale and he seemed focused in on himself.

Dido went over to Ollie's table and sat down. Neither of them spoke. They were both experiencing a sadness that seeped into everything, making the concourse look mean and dingy.

Dido said, 'When will you be back?'

'I don't know,' said Ollie. 'I could be gone so long that you'll forget all about me.'

'No, I won't.'

Ollie slowly reached across the table and took Dido's hand.

'I hope not,' he said. 'I'm not going to forget you. Leaving's made me realise how much you mean to me.'

A noise came from the direction of the platforms, an insistent, rattling whine that increased in volume.

'My train's pulling in,' said Ollie.

Dido frowned, said, 'That's no train!' and woke up.

The dream faded, leaving behind the feeling of sadness and a loud whining sound that seemed to be coming from outside.

Dido checked the time on her radio-alarm – 05:45.

Who's making that racket at this hour? she wondered.

Cosmo, who'd spent the night curled up at the foot of Dido's bed, was evidently wondering the same thing. She'd jumped on to the window ledge and was half in, half out of the drawn curtains, lashing her tail and twittering furiously.

'Hey, less of the language!' said Dido.

She rolled out of bed, stepped over to the window,

pulled back the curtains and looked outside.

Mr Morrison, the Nesbits' next-door neighbour, was mowing his lawn into immaculately straight stripes. His face was flushed, and slick with sweat.

Dido was astonished. Mr Morrison was a widowed pensioner who kept himself to himself. The Nesbits hardly ever heard a peep from him. In fact he was so quiet that Dad sometimes called around to make sure that he was all right. Dido knew that Mr Morrison was a keen gardener, but mowing the lawn at a quarter to six in the morning went beyond keen to downright peculiar.

Mr Morrison paused, took a handkerchief from his trouser pocket and mopped his forehead. He spotted Dido at the window, beamed at her and waved.

Dido automatically waved back, though she felt more like heaving a brick.

Cosmo trilled enquiringly.

'What, feed you – right now?' said Dido.

Cosmo patiently explained that, for cats, there was nothing like a hard night's sleep for building up an appetite, and they were so worn out by the effort of eating that they needed to go back to sleep as soon as they'd finished.

Dido gave in and let Cosmo lead the way downstairs.

Dad was in the kitchen, standing over the electric kettle which wheezed and popped as it heated. Cosmo sprang on to the work surface and head-butted Dad's arm.

'You're awake early,' said Dido.

'I didn't have much of a choice,' Dad growled. 'Old Charlie's lawnmower ruined my beauty sleep.'

'Don't worry, Dad. The beauty sleep wasn't working anyway.'

Dad ignored the crack and said, 'I don't get what Charlie's playing at. He's usually so considerate.'

'Why don't you ask him?'

'I already did. I asked him what he was doing, and d'you know what he said?'

'Er, "I'm mowing my lawn'?"suggested Dido.

'No, he told me he had to get ready.'

'Get ready for what?'

'A visitor, I think. He was a bit garbled.'

'What visitor?' said Dido. 'Mr Morrison never gets visitors.'

'Well he's mowing his lawn for somebody.'

'Maybe he's got a hot date with someone from the Over-Sixties Club.'

Cosmo jumped off the work surface, padded to the cupboard where the cat food was kept, probed the edge of the door with her claws, prised it open and yowled.

'What's she complaining about?' said Dad.

'The standard of service,' Dido said. 'She wants to know why we're standing around talking when we could be feeding her and talking.'

Dad looked down at Cosmo.

'Knock it off, feline!' he said. 'This house doesn't revolve around you, you know.'

Even a beginner in Cat would have recognised Cosmo's reply as, 'Oh no?'

When Dido left the house to catch the bus to school, she stopped at the end of the drive because her thumbs were itching. Itchy thumbs was always a sign from her magic that something was wrong. Dido looked around to see if she could spot what it was.

Nothing struck her at first. Mistletoe Lane was peaceful and tidy.

Wait a minute, thought Dido. Isn't it a little *too* tidy?

Garden hedges had been trimmed, grass cut,

windows polished, paintwork cleaned, cars washed until they gleamed. The street was as perfect and unreal as a set in a TV ad.

Dido used her inseeing. Magic intensified her senses, giving colours a taste and quiet a touch. Her own house, guarded by protection spells, was a web of multicoloured filaments that seethed and shimmered. The other houses were fizzing with bubbles that winked as they burst. Dido felt the neighbourhood waiting with an excitement that bordered on agitation. It reminded her of going to a pantomime with Mum and Dad when she was little. The audience, mostly toddlers, had got so out of hand that there had almost been a riot.

Excitement? thought Dido. In *Stanstowe*?

It was puzzling, but there was no time to get to the bottom of it; if she didn't get a move on, she was going to miss her bus.

Scott wasn't looking his best when Dido joined him at the bus stop. His hair was lank, his eyes were bleary and he kept yawning.

'Rough night?' said Dido.

'Didn't get much sleep. I was too hot,' Scott said. 'I heard Mum get up at four, so I got up as well. I helped her clean the house.'

'*Huh?*'

Scott shrugged.

'It needed doing,' he said. 'The place hasn't been dusted for a fortnight. I scrubbed the porch too. It was worth it though.'

'Why?'

'Because now everything's ready.'

'Ready?' said Dido.

Scott seemed surprised at her reaction.

'Yeah,' he said. 'Haven't you heard? The Queen's coming to Stanstowe.'

'And she's going to your house?'

Scott's forehead wrinkled.

'Was it the Queen?' he said. 'Some big-shot's coming anyway. It was on the radio.'

'When?'

'First thing this morning. Or was it the TV? I can't remember.'

Dido was concerned. Scott seemed unusually vague, as though something was interfering with his memory.

'Scott,' she said, as tactfully as she could manage, 'didn't it strike you as weird to get up before dawn and do the housework?'

Scott's eyes narrowed.

'Are you saying my mum is weird?' he demanded gruffly.

'No, I—'

'Considering you and your family, calling my family weird is pretty funny, isn't it?'

Dido could tell that they were going down a dangerous road, and she did some nifty backing-down.

'You're right,' she said. 'I'm sorry. I know how busy your mum must be. I guess she has to fit housework in where she can.'

'Mmm,' said Scott, and Dido took it that her apology had been accepted.

After registration Dido's form, Nine North, went down to the Main Hall for upper-school assembly. The headmaster, Dr Parker, swept on to the stage, wearing a black academic gown that made him resemble an overgrown fruitbat. He had a determined expression on his face.

'I've received news that the school is to be inspected by an extremely eminent person,' he announced, his voice filling the hall. 'So imagine my disappointment when I arrived this morning and saw how untidy we've become. There's litter in every corner of every playground, and the fence at the edge of the playing fields is festooned with crisp packets and sweet wrappers. This casts a poor light on us as a community. I've decided that since we're responsible for making the mess, it's also our responsibility to deal with it. Teaching will be suspended during First Lesson. I expect the whole school to turn out for litter duty. We must make ourselves ready.'

Dido caught her breath. First Mr Morrison, then the other neighbours, then Scott, now Dr Parker. The whole town seemed to be getting ready for somebody, without being exactly certain who the somebody was.

This is crazy! thought Dido. Is it just me, or has everyone flipped?

From behind her, Dido heard Jack Farmer saying, 'The Doc's dead right. This school's a tip. It'll be much better when it's cleaned up, won't it?'

'It isn't just me,' Dido whispered to herself. 'The heat's fried everyone's brains.'

5
Black Bones

John laced his way through the clog of the early morning rush hour. Some of the guys at work took the mick out of his scooter, and if he happened to pass one of them, stuck in a long tailback at a set of traffic lights, he made a point of giving them a cheery wave.

He arrived at the DIY store with enough time to spare to make himself a cup of coffee in the staffroom before changing into his overalls and reporting to Harry, his supervisor.

Harry was in the paint section.

'What's the drill this morning, Harry?' said John.

Harry jerked his thumb towards an industrial-strength vacuum cleaner that almost blocked the aisle.

'That is, my son,' he said.

'Eh?'

'The manager's having kittens. He'd heard that

some big director's coming down from London to carry out a random inspection. He wants the place spotless. Your job is to vacuum the cutting room.'

'But it hasn't been vacuumed in years!' said John. 'There's sawdust everywhere. It'll take me hours.'

'Yours is not to reason why, my son,' Harry said. 'Hop to it.'

Cursing and grumbling, John hopped. Before long he was making the acquaintance of corners of the cutting room that he hadn't even known existed.

As he worked, John thought about Bivco – couldn't get him out of his mind. Funny thing was though, the more John thought about it, the more last night seemed like a dream.

It had been OK at the start. Bivco had produced a half bottle of vodka, and they'd sat in the circle and shared it, talking over the things they'd got up to when they'd been pupils at Prince Arthur's. John reached the woozy stage and was about to suggest calling it a night, when Bivco started flashing pills around, saying that it was great gear he'd scored in a London club.

John cried off, told Bivco that the top of Stanstowe Hill was no place for anyone to get out of their skulls.

It didn't stop Bivco. He popped three pills and washed them down with the last of the vodka. Then he *really* started talking, jabbering about out-there stuff that made John wonder if his old mate wasn't a couple of strings of bunting short of a street party. John gave up listening in the end and watched in disgusted fascination as white flecks of foam formed in the corners of Bivco's mouth. Bivco's eyes became empty, as if he'd vacated his body and somebody smaller had moved in.

John was seriously spooked. Bivco had turned into bad news, and John hoped he wasn't carrying a knife along with the pills and vodka.

Luckily, Bivco zonked just before midnight. John checked that his breathing was all right, turned him on his side so that he wouldn't choke if he puked in his sleep, and left him at the circle. He didn't particularly want to see Bivco again and didn't expect to – not if he saw Bivco first anyway.

When lunchtime finally arrived, John left the store. He'd once chanced on a bench by the river, almost concealed by a raised bed of flowering shrubs at the far end of the car park. No one else seemed to know the bench was there. It was a perfect spot to get away from everybody and chill. If he was in the mood, John chucked the crusts of his sandwiches into the river, for the ducks and swans.

John had just taken a bite out of his second round of cheese and chutney, when a shadow fell across him. He looked up, saw Bivco grinning down at him, and the mouthful of sandwich was transformed into cement and wallpaper paste.

'I thought I'd find you here, Johnno,' Bivco said. 'Mind if I sit down?'

'Course not,' said John, lying. He shifted over to make room.

Bivco didn't look like someone who'd spent the night in the open. He was dressed all in black, right down to his boots and right up to the lenses and frames of his shades. His hair was gelled up into spikes and he was clean-shaven.

'How?' said John.

'How what?'

'Did you know I'd be here?'

'It's not that hard to find people, Johnno,' said Bivco. He spread his arms out over the back of the bench and stared at the river.

A silence stretched out until it was ominous.

To break it, John said, 'Quite a coincidence, bumping into each other like that last night.'

'No coincidence, Johnno,' Bivco said darkly.

'What d'you mean?'

'We were drawn together.'

'You reckon?'

'It's the power of the circle, Johnno. We felt it when we were kids, and it hasn't gone away.'

Bivco was getting creepy again, and John shuddered.

'Look, Biv,' he said, 'it was great meeting up with you, but to be honest, I wasn't drawn anywhere. It was a spur of the moment thing, you know? I was at a loose end last night, and—'

'The idea of going to the Speaking Stones just popped into your head,' Bivco interrupted. 'Right out of the blue. That's the way it works, Johnno.' Bivco changed position and crouched forwards. 'See, for the last few months in the centre, I had these dreams.'

'Get away!' said John, wishing that Bivco would.

Bivco nodded.

'Only they were more than dreams. They were, like, real,' he said. 'I saw Him.'

John noticed the capital letter in Bivco's voice, and wondered if Bivco had got religion, become a happy-clappy merchant.

'Him?' John said.

'He who walks in the paths of Shadow,' said Bivco. 'He taught me a lot, Johnno. I understand now.'

'That's terrific, Biv!' John said, and thought, Oh no, he's going to give me a *sermon*!

'He was with us at the start, but we were too young to suss that. Those things we did years back were—'

'Leave it out, Biv!' John said uneasily. 'Let's face it, we were a couple of nerds who watched too many horror videos and read too many junky books. It was a stupid game.'

Bivco's smile made him look as placid as a statue of Buddha.

'That's what I used to think, Johnno, but I was hiding from the truth, and so are you. He's real – always has been – and He's on his way.'

'On his way where?'

'Into the world,' said Bivco. 'There are going to be changes, Johnno. Big changes. I have to show people the way.'

'Biv,' John said gently. 'Those pills you had on you last night. How long have you been taking them?'

Bivco laughed.

'You don't get it, do you, Johnno?' he said. 'You think I'm spaced out, right? Well, I'll prove I'm not. Watch this!'

Bivco bunched his left hand into a fist, held it out and slowly opened his fingers.

Bivco's hand caught light. Between the purple flames, John could see sinews and black bones. Bivco didn't seem to be in any pain, and his mouth was stretched into a smug smile.

John's jaw dropped.

'How d'you do that?' he gasped.

'It's one of the things He showed me.'

'What's the trick?'

'The trick,' said Bivco, 'is to believe.'

6
Pressure

Litter duty had been no picnic. After forty-five minutes in the blazing sunshine, most of the pupils in Prince Arthur's were worn out, and by lunchtime the school was practically comatose.

Dido, Philippa, Scott and Ollie met up in the cafeteria, which was as quiet as a church. Dido didn't feel much like eating. She searched her salad to find a tasty bit, but when she saw that the pile of grated cheese on the side of her plate had dried out until it resembled earwax, she gave up pretending to be hungry and observed her friends.

Only Ollie seemed to have an appetite. Like Dido, Philippa and Scott were just toying with their food.

'Oh, gross!' Ollie said. 'The chocolate's melted on this KitKat.' He held it up for the others to inspect. 'It looks like the inside of a baby's nappy, doesn't it?'

Philippa set down her knife and fork with a clatter.

'Thanks so much for sharing that with us while we're eating, Ollie!' she snapped.

Scott scowled at her.

'And thank you so much for bawling down my ear, Philippa,' he said.

'I was *not* bawling,' said Philippa. 'You want me to show you bawling?'

Ollie wiggled his eyebrows at Dido and said, 'Want to share this KitKat with me? It's too messy to eat with our fingers, but we can use straws.'

'That's it!' Philippa announced, standing up. 'I'm going to find somewhere quiet and shady, where I can dissolve in peace. Coming, Dido?' She shot Dido a meaningful look.

'Um, yeah, sure!' said Dido.

She and Philippa binned their leftovers, stacked their plates and cutlery, and went outside.

Reflected heat struck Dido like a slap in the face. The humid air was heavy, and breathing in felt as though she were inhaling someone else's breath. Everyone was wilting – even Year Seven boys couldn't summon up the energy to yell and tear around – and shade was in great demand. All the best spots had already been taken. Dido and Philippa traipsed around for several minutes before discovering a welcome pocket of shadow beside one of the temporary classrooms on the lawn outside C Block. They sat on the grass.

'I can't take much more of this!' said Philippa. 'We need a thunderstorm to clear the air.'

'What's up?' Dido said.

'Huh?'

'You didn't drag me out here to discuss the weather, did you? Is it Scott?' said Dido, mentally adding – again.

To Dido's surprise, Philippa said, 'No, but it is sort of a girlie thing. I'm worried about Alison.'

'Why?'

'Well, you know the baby's due in six weeks? Alison should be taking things easy.'

'But she isn't?'

Philippa plucked a blade of grass and rolled it into a pill between the tips of her thumb and index finger.

'She's doing way too much,' she said. 'You're clued-up on stuff, Dido. I know pregnant women have morning sickness and cravings for peculiar food, but do they ever go loopy?'

'Loopy in what way?'

'I woke up at five this morning with a raging thirst, so I went downstairs for a glass of water,' said

Philippa. 'Alison was on her hands and knees in the kitchen, washing the floor. When I told her she shouldn't, she said she had to get things ready. I think she meant for the baby.'

'Nest-building?' Dido said.

Philippa nodded.

'I'm wondering how much else she'd been doing on the quiet,' she said. 'I know I ought to tell Dad about it, but—'

'You don't want to grass Alison up.'

'Right.'

'I wouldn't stress,' said Dido. 'Alison isn't going gaga. The Head's been bitten by the cleaning bug too.'

Philippa drew her lips into a cross pout.

'That was completely out of order!' she fumed. 'He used us as slaves. Someone ought to write to the Human Rights Commission.'

'Not everybody minded,' Dido pointed out. 'The Terrible Trio certainly got stuck in, didn't they?'

'I *so* couldn't believe the way they acted!' said Philippa. 'If I didn't know them better, I'd say they were sucking up to Dr Parker. They weren't the only ones either. It was like half the school was moaning about having to do litter duty, and the other half enjoyed it.'

Dido's thumbs tingled. Philippa seemed to have hit a nail bang on the head – but which nail?

The sound of raised voices made both girls turn their heads.

A group of Year Sevens – girls and boys – had gathered in a tight circle outside the entrance to C Block. In the centre of the circle was a short, skinny boy, and all his body language screamed out, Victim! His head hung down, his arms were held tightly against his sides and he writhed as the circle jostled him this way and that.

'Josh-ua's a los-er! Josh-ua's a los-er!'

Dido got to her feet and straightened her skirt.

'Where are you off to?' Philippa asked.

'To sort that lot out before things turn nasty,' said Dido.

'Oh, leave them alone. They're just mucking about.'

But Dido couldn't leave them alone. It was in her nature to protect the weak, partly because she was a Light Witch, and mostly because she was Dido. She marched over to the group and said, 'Hey, cut it out, will you? What's your problem?'

'Haven't got a problem,' said a girl with fair hair, wide blue eyes and a butter-wouldn't-melt face. She wrinkled her cute nose. 'Joshua's the one with a problem – a big problem.'

The rest of the group laughed scornfully.

'And that would be?' said Dido.

'He's not like us.'

'He's not?'

'We all support Man United, and Joshua's a *Chelsea* fan.' The fair-haired girl made it sound as if Chelsea fans tortured kittens for kicks.

'So?' said Dido.

The fair-haired girl narrowed her eyes.

'What team d'you support then?' she said threateningly.

Dido glanced around the circle and saw the same dangerous look in every eye. The group was one animal with six heads.

'That's none of your business,' said Dido. 'Buzz off before I report you to a teacher.'

'I don't think you want to do that,' said the fair-haired girl. 'I think that would be really stupid, don't you?'

Dido became uncomfortably aware that the circle had widened and that she was now inside it. It seemed that there was going to be a scuffle, and Dido was anxious to avoid it because she didn't want anyone to get hurt – least of all herself. Without her calling on it, Dido's magic produced an intimidation spell. In her imagination, a black mountain erupted, sending out a vast plume of yellowish-grey smoke and glowing streams of molten rock. Red-hot chunks the size of family cars showered down, exploding like bombs when they hit the ground.

The group saw Dido expand, growing taller, more and more powerful. She radiated menace. The circle split, and turned back into a bunch of Year Sevens, blinking sheepishly at one another, wondering how they'd managed to get themselves into such a tricky situation.

The tense silence was broken by chimes.

The fair-haired girl's tough-little-cookie act vanished.

'It's the ice-cream van!' she squealed. 'Let's go, gang!'

The group scattered like the fragments of a china plate dropped on to a tiled floor.

The volcano in Dido's mind vanished.

That was too much, Dido thought. I didn't need magic for that, I could have talked them down.

Once again, her magic had acted outside her control.

Joshua lifted his head. He had curly ginger hair and dark, adoring eyes.

'Thanks,' he said.

'You're welcome,' said Dido. 'Do they always pick on you like that?'

'No. They're my friends. One second we were having a laugh, next second they were calling me names.'

'Guess you shouldn't have mentioned football, eh?'

'I didn't,' said Joshua. 'I didn't mention anything about anything.'

'If they pick on you again, go grab a teacher or a prefect, OK?'

Joshua smiled.

'What's your name?' he said.

'Dido.'

'I think you're brilliant!'

'You know that and I know that, but don't tell anyone else,' Dido joked. 'I'll get a reputation for being a goody!'

That evening, Mum came home while Dido and Dad were watching the early news on TV. She dropped herself into an armchair, grunted, stuck out her bottom lip and blew air upwards over her face.

'Good day?' said Dad.

'No, a pig of a day!' Mum snarled. 'Alan Parker had a bee in his bonnet about litter, and he used the pupils as unpaid litter cleaners. I warned him that we'd get complaints from parents, but would he listen?'

'Perhaps he's having a mid-life crisis.'

'He's having something!' Mum muttered darkly.

'Hey, can we have a little more quiet, please?' said Dido. 'I want to catch the weather forecast.'

The weather forecaster was a young woman. She spouted the usual guff about anticyclones and rainfall figures, then pasted on a smile with too many teeth in it and said, 'But it's bad news for the people of Stanstowe, I'm afraid. They've been enjoying a spell of unusually fine weather, with long hours of sunshine and temperatures well above the seasonal average. However, their run of good fortune is about to come to a dramatic end.' She waved her hand over a long, thick line on the left of the map of Britain. 'A low pressure system is headed across the Atlantic, and it's reported to be a particularly nasty one, with high winds and low temperatures, so Stanstowe should be back to normal in a day or so.'

'Thank goodness for that!' said Dad. 'Another week of this heat and people will be climbing the walls.'

'Back to normal?' Mum mused. 'Now there's something to look forward to.'

High above the Atlantic at 02:30 Greenwich Mean Time, BA flight 118 from Heathrow to New York JFK ran into turbulence. The turbulence was caused by a weather front that the pilot, Captain Sawyer, had already climbed to avoid, but the front had grown far faster that the Met Office's estimate. The aircraft lurched like a bus on a bumpy road, then bucked and snaked. It felt as though the aeroplane was being mauled by a gigantic and invisible cat. Captain Sawyer turned off the autopilot and resumed manual control.

In the passenger section, people woke and stared at one another; some prayed. A violent wrench burst open the doors of the overhead lockers, raining down their contents. A stewardess, fighting to maintain her balance and to keep her voice calm, made an announcement over the intercom.

'As the aircraft is currently experiencing heavy turbulence, all passengers are advised to stay in their seats and fasten their safety belts until conditions improve.'

Outside the aeroplane, the wings and control surfaces fluttered. Fingers of ice began to creep over the metal. The engines shrieked in the thin air as the pilot opened the throttles wide to gain height.

At last, the machine steadied. Captain Sawyer and his co-pilot exchanged sighs of relief.

Below them, in the moonlight, a vast purple cloud stretched out like a dark country in the sky. Towering thunderheads pulsed with lightning.

'What is *that?*' the co-pilot asked in awe.

'That,' said Captain Sawyer, 'is the Mother of Storms.'

7
Sacrifice

Dido was fast asleep. To stay as cool as possible, she'd stretched out on top of her duvet, and was lying on her left side, breathing evenly.

Cosmo padded her paw against the sole of Dido's left foot until Dido reflexively jerked her knee and woke herself up.

'Huh?' mumbled Dido.

Cosmo answered her with a long string of purrs and growls that Dido wasn't awake enough to follow.

'What light?' she said, sitting up. 'Of course it's getting light – it's called morning.'

Cosmo said something equally as sarcastic in return.

Dido looked at the clock and saw that Cosmo was right. Though dawn was still hours away, her bedroom was lit by a soft grey radiance that wasn't coming from the window. The source of the light was on a bookshelf, fixed to the wall opposite the bed.

Dido's crystal ball was glowing.

Her parents had given her the ball as a present on her thirteenth birthday, her Covening, when she'd come of age as a Light Witch. Dido used the ball as a Spirit Mirror, a way of keeping in touch with her magic. Now, it seemed, her magic was attempting to get in touch with her.

Dido got up, took down the crystal ball and returned to the bed, sitting on the edge of the mattress, cradling the ball in her cupped hands. The light turned her fingers a translucent red. Every now and then, jagged white sparks like miniature lightning flickered through the crystal. Dido timed the flashes, found their rhythm and let it fill her body.

Dim shapes filled the room, as thin and patchy as film projected on to smoke. The edges of the shapes grew more definite, then leapt out sharply, and Dido suddenly wasn't in her bedroom.

She was at the centre of her magic, in a forest clearing, at the edge of a pool. The pool was fed by a spring that tumbled over a pile of stones, the water glittering in the bright sunshine. Seated cross-legged on the grass beside the pool was someone Dido had met before – Lilil, the spirit of her magic.

Lilil appeared to be the same age as Dido, but was thousands of years old, having been reborn in countless Light Witches over the centuries. Lilil was wearing a puffy-sleeved top and britches that were the same shade of dove grey as her eyes. Or was it *his* eyes? Lilil's shock of white-blonde curls looked feminine, but Lilil's hands were large, like a man's. Nothing about Lilil was straightforward, least of all his/her smile, which managed to be both wise and mischievous.

'Which are you this time,' said Dido, 'a boy or a girl?'

'Both. Neither. Does it matter?' Lilil said.

'I guess not. So, Lilil, what's the story?'

Lilil frowned and said, 'I know an eternity of stories. Which would you like me to tell?'

Dido sighed. It was always like this with Lilil. If you didn't ask precisely the right question, Lilil avoided giving an answer.

'I meant that you must have called me here for a reason,' said Dido.

'That's correct.'

Dido waited for Lilil to go on. When Lilil didn't, Dido said, 'Why did you call me here?'

'The sign in the sky.'

Dido automatically looked overhead. There was nothing in the sky.

Lilil laughed. 'Not that sky, Dido. The sky in your world.'

It didn't take long for Dido to work out what Lilil was talking about, it had been all over the newspapers and TV for weeks.

'You mean the comet?' she said.

'Do I?'

Dido's temper flared.

'Lilil, can we skip the games and get to the point?' she demanded. 'Are you telling me that Comet Bailey-Hooper is a sign?'

'Yes.'

'A sign of what?'

'The Time of the Stars has come,' said Lilil. 'Spelkor is waking.'

A band of ice tightened around Dido's chest. Sometimes she'd gone for days without thinking about Spelkor, the god of Shadow Magic. He'd been trapped inside Stanstowe Hill when the Speaking Stones were erected. Light Witch legend said that at the Time of the Stars he would free himself, and the world would be thrown into chaos.

'Are you sure?' said Dido, hoping against hope.

'Would you be here if I wasn't?'

'Has he been causing the trouble in Stanstowe? Is that what everybody's getting ready for?'

'His strength is growing,' said Lilil. 'But don't despair, Dido. Your fate and Spelkor's are bound together.'

'Is that why my magic's been acting up? Just recently it's been getting way out of line.'

'Your magic has changed. You are no longer a Light Witch,' Lilil said. 'At your Covening, the Light and Shadow Magic in you reunited into Twilight Magic. You are the first Twilight Witch your world has seen for thousands of years, and your power is growing. The Time of the Stars will be your time too.'

The fact that Dido was a Twilight Witch seemed to make sense of all the things that had been happening with her magic lately, but she didn't see how it would help her in her struggle with Spelkor.

'Yeah, sure!' she said. 'I have a showdown with the bad guy, whip his butt and we all live happily ever after. The fact that he's an all-powerful god and I'm a fourteen-year-old schoolgirl doesn't come into it.'

Lilil stared at the ripples on the surface of the pool

and said, 'I share your fears, Dido, but fear is not the answer.'

'Then what is?'

'Acceptance. Spelkor is far mightier than you, but he's not all-powerful. He has flaws and weakness that can be worked on.'

'How?'

'Watch over those who are close to you and protect them when you must, but otherwise don't fight the Shadow One.'

Dido was bewildered. She'd been expecting to fight Spelkor and had thought that she was the only person who stood a chance against him. Alone among Light Witches, she'd been permitted to study Shadow Magic. If she couldn't defeat Spelkor, what had been the point of her long hours of learning?

'Don't fight him?' she said.

'You know the paths of Shadow. Use that knowledge.'

'What do I do, give him a kiss on both cheeks and tell him how great it is to see him?'

Lilil turned to Dido, and Dido saw that Lilil's eyes were grave.

'This is no joke, Dido. You must offer him something that he dearly wants but cannot have,'

Lilil said. 'It will demand a great sacrifice from you, but it's the only way. The alternative is to be Spelkor's slave and join him in inflicting suffering upon millions.'

Dido didn't like the sound of 'sacrifice'. It conjured up pictures of altar stones and double-edged knives.

'What kind of sacrifice?' she said.

'One that's given freely and willingly,' said Lilil. 'You'll know it when the hour comes.'

A terrifying thought roared through Dido's mind and burst out of her mouth.

'Am I going to die, Lilil?' she said. 'Will Spelkor kill me – is that the sacrifice I have to make?'

'You'll know,' said Lilil.

Lilil, the boulders and the forest lost their colour as they flowed into themselves and the pool. The pool rounded itself and shrank into the ball of crystal in Dido's hands. The light in the crystal faded.

Dido kept her eyes fixed on the ball, desperately wishing that it would send her a different message. Despite the warmth of the bedroom, her legs were trembling and her teeth chattered.

Cosmo mewed supportively.

'I know, Coz,' said Dido, reaching out to scratch the top of the cat's head. 'I'm there for you as well. I couldn't get through any of this without you.'

It was a lie, intended to comfort them both. The truth was, Dido had to face something without knowing if she could get through it at all.

The party broke up around two. John was among the last to leave. He hadn't particularly wanted to go in the first place, but a funny feeling had told him that if he stayed in, Bivco would've turned up again, and that might have been more than John could have handled. He'd shown John some stuff that John couldn't explain, and didn't want to explain. John led a nice, safe, boring life and he preferred to keep it that way. Halfway home, the engine on John's scooter died. John fiddled with the ignition and the spark plugs, then realised that he'd run out of petrol. He cursed himself for not filling up earlier, and thought for a bit. Home was six kilometres away, and it was four kilometres to the nearest twenty-four-hour service station. Either meant a long walk, slowed down by having to push the scooter. If that wasn't bummer enough, the weather had taken a turn for the worse. When John exhaled he could see his breath, and it was getting colder by the second.

Yeah, that'd be right! John said to himself. The old Loomis luck strikes again.

A jet passed overhead, flying unusually low. John glanced up at it, and saw something weird. A massive bank of cloud was seething across the sky, moving at an incredible speed. John watched in fascination as the cloud swallowed the moon and stars. The wind picked up, chilly enough to make John shiver. There was no point in hanging about. The faster he walked, the warmer he'd be and the sooner he'd get home. John seized the scooter's handlebars and pushed.

Three minutes later, snow started falling. Thick flakes flurried in the wind, coiling themselves into tubes that snaked over the tarmac of the road. A flake burst against John's eyelashes, splitting the light from the street lamps into rainbows. What was going on with the weather? It had been boiling all day, now it was like the Arctic.

At the junction of Sycamore Lane and Elm Close, John paused. He could go the long way by sticking to the main drag, but the cold was already getting a grip. It felt like his fingernails were being squeezed by pliers. The smart thing would be to take a short cut through Chiggle's Wood.

Chiggle's Wood wasn't much of a wood, just a

copse of straggly birch trees on a patch of land that had survived the building of a 1970s housing estate. Couples made out there, though John seriously doubted that anyone would be making out tonight. Problem was, the wood was unlit. Not that John was afraid of the dark, of course, but he didn't fancy losing his footing and landing face down in a pile of pooch flop.

A freezing blast of wind made John's mind up for him. He steered the scooter off the pavement, on to the path that led into the trees.

It was kind of creepy in Chiggle's Wood. The path twisted and was difficult to follow. Every so often there was a noise that made John jump – a rustle, like something dropping into the undergrowth. John couldn't make head or tail of it, until something small and round bounced on to the path, right in front of him. He crouched down to investigate.

It was a dead sparrow. The sudden plunge in temperature had been too much for it. All round John, small birds were dying, tumbling frozen from their roosts. John shuddered and walked on at a brisker pace. He didn't like being around any kind of death.

Then, unexpectedly, John met death full on. His

foot caught on what felt like a tree root and he stumbled. He swore and looked down. A hand and arm lay across the path. Somebody was stretched out in a clump of bracken, a tramp, by the look of the clothes.

'You all right, mate?' John said.

Dumb question, because anybody who had to sleep rough on a snowy night obviously wasn't all right.

There was no response. Even in the darkness, John could see that the skin on the hand was an unhealthy colour, and the fingers were clenched into a claw.

'Hello?' said John.

Gingerly he bent down, keeping the scooter steady with his left hand and touched the wrist. It was stone cold and he couldn't detect any pulse. He was alone in the middle of Chiggle's Wood, with a stiff.

John's heartbeat pounded in his ears, and he teetered on the edge of panic. What to do, go home and contact emergency services, or leg it and leave the corpse for someone else to find?

As John was trying to decide, the tramp spoke.

'It'll happen to you one day, you know,' he said. 'It happens to everybody.'

John laughed in shock.

'You nearly gave me a heart attack, mate!' he said.

'You were so quiet, I thought you were dead.'

'I am dead,' said the tramp.

'You what?'

'I am dead,' the tramp said again.

John knew the guy must be a psycho and ought to be humoured, but couldn't resist saying, 'Yeah? I thought dead people couldn't talk.'

'All that's about to change,' said the dead tramp.

John lost it. He let go of the scooter and bolted.

8
Shapes in the Snow

Philippa lay on her back, suspended midway between sleep and consciousness. She heard noises downstairs – the clink and rattle of plates and mugs, the snap of the dishwasher door, the electronic burble of a local radio station's jingle – and there was a tightness in her bladder that she'd have to get up and do something about before long, but the noises seemed unconnected with her. For the moment, she was enjoying letting her mind drift.

Then, gradually, she became aware of another sound. When she concentrated and tried to isolate it, the sound slipped away, but it returned as soon as she relaxed – a faint voice, scratchy as an old vinyl recording.

'*...ready ... you must make ready ... you must make ready ...*'

Philippa's bedroom door crashed open, shocking her awake. Her brother Tom stood in the doorway. He was in his pyjamas and dressing gown, and his eyes were bright with excitement.

'Have you seen it?' he gabbled. 'Isn't it great? School's closed early. It's just been on the radio, we've got an extra week's holiday!'

'Tom,' said Philippa, 'what are you on about?'

'Take a look out the window. I'm going to get dressed and help Dad. Are you coming?'

'Maybe – once I've woken up properly. Now go away and close the door, but don't sla—'

Tom slammed the door before Philippa could finish telling him not to. She muttered under her breath, then noticed for the first time how cold her room was. Philippa rolled out of bed, wrapped the duvet around her shoulders, went to the window and peeped through the curtains. The peep stretched out into a long stare.

'Oh, wh-a-a-t?' Philippa gasped.

The street outside had been transformed by a layer of snow almost a metre thick. The white hummocks on the drive directly below must be Dad's car and Alison's runaround, Philippa guessed, and the row of short twigs protruding from the surface of the snow on the front lawn was all she could see of the rose bushes.

All the rest was white-out.

Philippa felt a twinge of delight, a throwback to her younger days when she'd considered snow as a free toy. The twinge deepened into sharp discomfort as her bladder sent her an urgent message. She turned from the window and made a dash to the bathroom.

When Philippa went downstairs, Dad was in the hall, struggling to put on a pair of wellingtons.

'What's going on, Dad?' Philippa enquired.

Dad's reply bristled with sarcasm.

'The heatwave appears to have ended,' he said. 'We're snowed in at the front, and guess who's going to have to dig us out?'

'What about your meeting in London today?'

'Strangely enough, Philippa, I've had to cancel my meeting. Perhaps all the snowdrifts blocking the roads will give you a clue as to why.'

'I was only asking, Dad. There's no need to get ratty.'

Dad rolled his eyes.

'You're right!' he said. 'I should be grateful. Shovelling the snow away from the front door is only going to be tedious and time-consuming.'

Tom came down the stairs two at a time, leaning

against the banister.

'OK, Dads!' he said. 'Let's get to it!'

Dad glared.

'Tom,' he said, 'don't get me wrong, I'm grateful for your help, but I find your enthusiasm a bit grating. Save your energy for the shovel.'

'Have fun, you two,' Philippa said, and ducked into the kitchen.

Alison was on tiptoes, rooting in the cupboard above the fridge-freezer. Her swollen stomach made her movements clumsy and awkward.

'Looking for something?' said Philippa.

'Checking,' Alison said.

'On what?'

'Things we need to stock up on, in case we can't get to the shops.'

'But if we can't get to the shops, how are we going to stock up?'

Alison went down on to the soles of her shoes and turned to face Philippa.

'Oh, I don't know!' she said irritably. 'Is there any loo cleaner left?'

'Pass.'

'I'd better go and find out.'

'But, Alison—'

'Not now, Philippa!' Alison snapped. 'Can't you see I'm busy?'

Philippa stepped aside to let Alison pass.

What's wrong with her this morning? Philippa thought. Snow or hormones?

Philippa made herself tea and a slice of toast, which she was still eating when the phone rang.

It was Ollie.

'How are things with you?' Ollie said.

'Snowy.'

'Yeah, it's the same all over town. My mum rang my grandparents in Buckley earlier. They don't have any snow. Looks like Stanstowe's going through its own personal Ice Age.'

'Lucky us!' grumbled Philippa. 'What are you going to do today?'

'Keep warm and survive, mostly. I don't think I'll be going anywhere much, and I can't watch TV.'

'Why not?'

'It's blacked out – major transmitter failure. Stuck in the house with no TV. Dream scenario, huh?'

'You could always talk to your parents.'

'Definitely not!' Ollie snorted. 'They've freaked. They're out in the garden with Steve, throwing snowballs at each other like a bunch of little kids.'

Philippa frowned. It didn't sound like the Mr and Mrs Falkener she knew, they were both reserved types.

'Dad and Alison are a bit peculiar as well,' Philippa said. 'I wonder what's causing it?'

'Adults!' said Ollie. 'Who knows why any of them act the way they do?'

Which was a fair point.

Mr Falkener paused, and dropped the snowball in his right hand. It landed with a soft thud.

'What was that again?' he said.

'You are wasting time,' said the voice. 'I have to be made, and you must make me. How can I exist without form?'

Mr Falkener looked at his wife and said, 'Did you hear that?'

'Yes,' she said.

Steve, Ollie's older brother, had heard the voice too.

'He's right,' he said. 'We have been wasting time.'

A movement in the garden next door caught Mrs Falkener's eye, and she half-turned. Little Henry was scooping together armfuls of snow, his face so intent that it was almost comical.

'What are you making, Henry?' Mrs Falkener called.

'A snowman,' Henry said. 'Only it's going to be a dinosaur, not a man.'

'What sort of dinosaur?'

Henry's forehead puckered. 'A stigga – a staggo—' he faltered. 'A big one, with all plates down his back.'

'You mean a Stegosaurus?' said Mrs Falkener.

Henry nodded, bouncing the bobble on top of his woollen hat.

'Can we help?'

'No!' said Henry. 'I have to do it by myself. He told me.'

'Who told you?'

'The dinosaur!' Henry said crossly.

Mr Falkener had a burst of inspiration.

'Steven,' he said, 'go and fetch Oliver. The more the merrier.'

As Steve struggled through the snow, Mrs Falkener said, 'That dinosaur of yours is going to have a friend, Henry.'

'Is he?'

'Yes. We're going to build a Tyrannosaurus Rex.'

'Oh, w-o-o-w!' said Henry.

*

After she'd finished talking to Ollie, Philippa showered and dressed. She decided that, given Alison's tetchiness, it would be better to stay out of her way, so she wrapped up warm, found her walking boots in the cupboard under the stairs, and went outside to give Dad and Tom a hand. Getting from the back of the house to the front proved to be a major trek. The snow came up over Philippa's knees, and every step crunched and squeaked.

Dad and Tom had cleared the snow from the front door, and piled it into an impressively large mound on the lawn. Tom was digging his way down the drive, his nose and lips blue with cold. Dad was gazing at the mound and seemed to be miles away.

'Have a break, Tom,' said Philippa. 'I'll take over.'

Tom didn't need to be told twice. He gave Philippa a thumbs-up sign, dropped his spade and trudged off towards the back door.

'What's the fascination, Dad?' said Philippa.

'Pardon?'

'A heap of snow is a heap of snow, isn't it?'

'Can you see a shape in it?' Dad said.

Philippa looked, and said, 'No, not really.'

'Concentrate,' said Dad. He pointed to a lump on top of the heap. 'That's a head, there are the eyes, and there's the nose.' He pointed lower down. 'There's a horse's hindquarters.'

Philippa looked closely at her father. He was obviously engrossed.

'Um, should I carry on with the drive?' she said, hoping that the question would break Dad's trance.

'Yes. I'll be with you in a minute.'

But Dad wasn't with her in a minute, or even ten minutes. Philippa slaved with the shovel while Dad stayed where he was, doing nothing.

By the time Philippa reached the bottom of the drive, she reckoned that she'd done her fair share, and the idea of a hot drink was attractive enough to be irresistible. She left her spade stuck in the snow and turned towards the house.

Dad was busy. He'd removed his gloves and was tearing frantically at the snow with his bare hands, carving it like a sculptor modelling clay.

'What are you doing?' Philippa said.

'Something important,' Dad grunted, 'so don't interrupt.'

Philippa took him at his word. She went into the house, knocked the snow off her boots and left them on the kitchen doormat, then filled and boiled a kettle, and poured the hot water over the contents of a sachet of drinking chocolate that she'd emptied into a mug. After stirring the chocolate, Philippa wrapped the fingers of both hands around the mug and carried it into the lounge.

Tom was in an armchair, playing a Nintendo game. The TV was on, but wasn't showing any programmes, just a printed announcement that read: *Transmission will be resumed as soon as possible.* A string orchestra sawed blandly away in the background.

Alison was at the window.

'What's your father up to?' she asked Philippa.

'Who knows?' said Philippa. 'He was rambling on about a shape in the snow – like a face and horse?'

Alison drew in a sharp breath.

'Oh, yes! I see!' she said.

The next thing Philippa knew, Alison had joined Dad on the lawn and was working at the snow with a trowel.

'Tom,' said Philippa, 'do Dad and Alison seem all right to you?'

'No, they're both a couple of grouchbags!' Tom said.

'They're making something.'

Tom shrugged.

'As long as they're not in here biting my head off, I don't care what they're doing,' he said sourly.

The television sprang into life.

'We apologise to viewers in the South for the break in transmission. This was due to severe weather conditions in the Stanstowe area. Now, a little later than scheduled, here's Carol Hudson with Friday Review.'

Daytime TV is rubbish! Philippa thought, but she settled down on the sofa to watch anyway.

Half an hour later, Dad came in. His anorak and trousers were soaked, his face and hands were mottled purple, but he wore a wide grin and his eyes were blissed-out.

'Come and see!' he said. 'You must come and see!'

'See what?' said Philippa.

'Hurry up!'

Dad chivvied Philippa and Tom outside.

There was a snow centaur on the lawn. Its face was twisted into a snarl, and its outstretched arms ended in clenched fists. Its body was rearing up on its hind legs, front hooves frozen in the act of slashing the air. The carving was far from perfect, but somehow its crudeness made it eerie.

Alison was standing beside the centaur. She

beamed at Philippa and Tom and said, 'Meet Chiron. Isn't he beautiful?'

'Er...yes,' said Philippa.

But Chiron wasn't beautiful, he was terrifying – and something was seriously wrong with Dad and Alison.

9
Closer than Blood

Dido was awake long before her alarm-radio went off at seven o' clock. She'd barely slept, only managing to doze now and then, and each time she'd woken, what Lilil had told her was still there. Fear loomed over her, its great dark jaws stretched wide.

To distract herself, Dido imagined how her life would be when she was grown-up. She'd make a career as a teacher, or maybe a doctor. She'd be married with two children, a girl and a boy, and their house would be—

The fantasy tailed off. The children were two-dimensional, like illustrations in a picture book, and her husband didn't have a face.

You can't see him because you might not have a future, Dido told herself.

Much to her surprise, she drew comfort from the thought. Nobody knew whether they had a future or not, just as nobody could be certain that any given day wouldn't be their last. But instead of giving up and curling into a ball of self-pity, most people brushed aside the idea of death and carried on with their lives.

'I've got to be like them,' Dido murmured. 'There are a lot more important things to be done than dying.' She remembered something that Lilil had said, and added, 'Fear is not the way.'

The panic that had threatened to overwhelm her subsided. She was Dido, alive and aware, and she was determined to remain alive and aware for as long as she could.

There was a knock at the bedroom door.

At the foot of the bed Cosmo stirred, opened an eye and mewed softly.

'Come in, Mum,' Dido said.

Mum opened the door. She was carrying a tray.

'How did you know it was me?' she said.

'Cosmo told me.'

'Oh,' said Mum, stepping over the threshold. 'I've brought you some juice and coffee. You might as well have a lie-in. There was a blizzard in the night. All the roads are closed.'

'What about school?'

'Closed until the start of summer term.' Mum placed a glass of orange juice and a mug of coffee on the bedside table. 'Honestly, I don't understand this weather we're having. I know global warming is affecting the climate, but this is ridiculous.'

Mum sounded brittle, and Dido knew why.

'You don't have to pretend, Mum,' she said.

'Pretend?'

'That you don't know it's the Time of the Stars,' said Dido.

Mum sat at the far end of the bed and scratched Cosmo between the ears.

'Your witch spirit told you?' she said.

Dido nodded.

'Mine too, and your father's,' said Mum. 'He's in the garden, digging a way through to the sanctuary so we can ask the Goddess for guidance.'

The sanctuary was a summer house at the end of the garden. The Nesbits used it to meditate and study magic.

'I think the Goddess has her own problems to deal with right now,' said Dido. 'Mum, what d'you know about sacrifices? My spirit told me that I'd have to make one.'

Mum's face became expressionless.

'I only know what I've read in legends,' she said. '"In the days of the Time of the Stars, the Giver will appear and offer up a sacrifice to the Shadow One." That's from the Prophecies of Asphodel.'

'And I'm the Giver?'

'Yes.'

All her mum's body language indicated that this was a subject she'd rather not talk about, but Dido was determined to find out everything that she could. 'Does Asphodel say what happens after the sacrifice?' she asked.

'I'm afraid not. Shadowmasters are the experts on sacrifices. Light Witches are forbidden to use them.'

'Pity,' said Dido. 'I was hoping there was a book I could look up some answers in.'

'We-ell ...' said Mum.

Dido sat up and leaned forward.

'Well?' she said.

'There's your father's grimoire.'

Dido had used Dad's grimoire – his book of spells – once. It had taken her to a place outside time, where she'd fought and defeated a Shadowmaster.

'But that only has Light Magic spells in it,' she said.

'Not necessarily,' said Mum. 'It depends on how you use it.'

'Huh?'

Mum thought for a moment, then said, 'You know how, when you're in a good mood, everything seems fresh and clean, but if you're sad, all you can see is mess and ugliness?'

'You mean if you're miserable on a sunny day, you don't notice the sunshine?'

'Exactly. It's almost the same with the grimoire. If you consult it on a Light Magic problem, it'll give you a Light Magic solution, but if you have a question about Shadow Magic—'

Dido was several steps ahead.

'The grimoire has a dark side?' she said.

'Grimoires are suitcases,' said Mum. 'You take out of them what you put in.'

Dido felt a spark of hope.

'D'you think it might help?' she said.

Mum shrugged.

'I don't see how it could do any harm,' she said. 'Unless... Dido, I know you've used Shadow Magic before, but can you keep it under control?'

Under normal circumstances, Dido would have come out with a flip and reassuring reply, but this was no time to keep anything hidden.

'I guess this is where I find out,' she said.

The pain in Dad's lower back demanded that he take a break. He gingerly straightened himself and took stock of his efforts. The path was still a few metres shy of the sanctuary, and his backache was going to get a lot worse before he was finished. Though the temptation to use magic was strong, Dad resisted it because Charlie was out in his garden and might spot him.

Dad had no idea what Charlie was doing, but Charlie's tuneless whistling had been getting on his nerves for nearly half an hour. Thinking that a neighbourly chat would provide a perfect excuse to put off work a little longer, Dad waded to the fence and looked over.

Charlie had built a figure out of snow. It was three metres high, a man with a wolf's head. The wolf's fangs were jaggedly broken twigs, and its eyes were pieces of flint.

Something cold crawled up Dad's spine.

'That's, um, an unusual sort of snowman, Charlie,' he said.

'It would be, if it was a snow*man*,' said Charlie, 'but it's not. It's a werewolf.'

'Don't you think it's a bit ...? I mean, if any little kids saw it, they might be frightened.'

'So they might,' Charlie said. 'But whoever heard of a friendly werewolf?'

'I...er...'

'What are you making?'

'Me? Nothing,' said Dad. 'I'm digging a path.'

Charlie's face darkened.

'You've not been told then,' he said.

'Told what?'

'He said it wasn't for everybody.'

'Who said?'

'The big feller,' said Charlie. 'The big feller from Stanstowe Hill.'

The coldness in Dad's spine reached the back of his skull and stimulated his inseeing with a suddenness that took him unawares.

Charlie was indistinct, a silhouette of violet fog, but the werewolf blazed, giving off a purple light that hurt Dad's eyes.

The werewolf shook its head, ran a snow tongue over its twig teeth.

'You are out of your depth, little man,' it said. 'Your kind is doomed.'

Charlie patted the werewolf on the back.

'That's right – you tell him,' he said.

The grimoire was in Dad's study, disguised as a computer manual. As Mum took it down from a shelf, she removed the spells protecting it, and the grimoire showed its true form, a book the size of a paperback, but as thick as a house brick. The black leather binding was cracked and scuffed, and the edges of the pages were greasy from thumbing.

Mum put the grimoire on to Dad's desk.

'How can I help?' she said.

'You can't,' said Dido. 'I have to be on my own for this one, Mum.'

Mum's smile was understanding, but her eyes showed disappointment.

'Fine! I'll leave you to it,' she said. 'Come on, Cosmo. Dido wants to be alone.'

Cosmo hissed the Cat for, 'No way!' and sprang on to the desk, purring as she rubbed her whiskers on the corners of the grimoire.

Mum laughed.

'First my daughter rejects me, then the family cat,' she said.

'I'm not rejecting you, Mum. I'm—'

'I know. You're protecting me,' said Mum. 'It was

my job to protect you before your Covening. Growing up is tough on parents, as well as children.' She laid a hand on Dido's shoulder and squeezed gently. 'Go with the Goddess,' she said.

After Mum had left, Dido let out a long breath.

'OK, what now?' she asked Cosmo. 'I never had to contact my Shadow Magic before, it was just sort of there when I needed it. What do I do?'

'Look at me!' Cosmo yowled. 'Look at m-e-e!'

Dido stared hard, saw the blue sheen on Cosmo's fur, the flecks and flakes in her amber eyes. A jolt of dangerous excitement shot through Dido, like the fearful thrill of a roller-coaster ride.

Cosmo grew. Her muscles swelled, her tail lengthened, her head and paws expanded until she was a sleek black panther, the spirit of Dido's Shadow Magic. The panther flicked its tail, sweeping the grimoire off the desk.

The grimoire tumbled as it fell. It flapped its covers and bobbed into the air, rising upwards, jerkily circling the panther's head.

The panther raised a paw, extended its claws and lashed out. Strips of shredded paper showered down like feathers.

The wounded grimoire slowly sank on to the desk,

landing upright with its covers open. The pages turned milkily opaque, then cleared. The book had changed into the frame of a window that looked into a different world.

A crone was seated at a table in a dusty, gloomy room. She was dressed in a filthy, ragged robe. She had wild white hair, a bony nose and thin lips that were pursed into a sour pout. Her face was shiny with ingrained dirt. She was flaying a rat, separating the skin from the flesh with a horny thumbnail.

The crone peered at Dido. Her squint was so severe that Dido didn't know which eye to look at.

'What do you want of me, Twilight Witch?' the crone demanded. 'And get a move on! My time's too precious to be wasted on the likes of you.'

Since the Shadow world didn't seem big on etiquette, Dido came straight to the point.

'In the days of the Time of the Stars, what sacrifice must the Giver offer to the Shadow One?' she said.

The crone grinned toothlessly.

'Ah, so that's it!' she gloated. 'That's why you've disturbed me with your prattling.'

'Do you know?'

The crone scowled.

'How could I possibly know, cretin?' she barked. 'Only the Giver knows what must be given, but I'll tell you this much ...' The crone's eyes rolled up, showing their yellowed whites, and she chanted in the voice of a far younger woman:

'Closer than blood and bone,
Hungry as fire,
Dearer than all you own,
Strong as desire,
Where strength and weakness are the same,
There love is hate, and loss is gain.'

She twitched and juddered, and her eyes rolled back.

'Is that it?' said Dido. 'What does it mean?'

The crone's eyes gleamed slyly. She snuffled and smacked her lips.

'You're afraid, Twilight Witch,' she cooed. 'How delicious!'

'Not afraid enough to stop me from doing what I have to do,' Dido said.

The crone flung the rat on to the table, wrapped her arms around herself and rocked backwards and forwards.

'You spoiled it!' she wailed. 'I haven't tasted the whisper of the echo of fear in four hundred years, and you have to spoil it! Begone – leave me!'

The window closed. Writing returned to the grimoire's pages and it toppled over.

Cosmo was Cosmo-sized again.

'A fat lot of use that was,' said Dido. 'I thought talking to Lilil was tricky, but that old bat talked total rubbish. And what was all that Twilight Witch stuff about?'

'No idea – but nice rat!' Cosmo purred.

It took Dido some time to replace the spells that protected the grimoire. They kept slipping off, and it was hard work to make them stick.

Maybe it's too soon after using Shadow Magic, Dido thought, but when she left the study and went to the top of the stairs, her witch senses told her that something was wrong.

The wrongness was stronger downstairs. It was creeping out of the lounge, gradually filling the house. Cautiously, Dido approached the lounge doorway.

Dad was stretched out on the sofa. His eyes were tightly shut and his skin was pale. Beads of sweat gathered on his forehead and trickled into his hair.

He thrashed his head from side to side, muttering under his breath.

Mum was cross-legged on the floor beside the sofa, holding Dad's hand.

Dido's thumbs itched and burned.

'Mum?' she said.

The worry in Mum's eyes made her look like a little girl.

'He's been touched by Spelkor, Dido,' she said.

'How did that happen?'

'I don't know. He came in twenty minutes ago in a terrible state, talking about a voice that was giving him orders. It was if he was struggling with himself – a part of him tried to resist the voice, but another part of him wanted to obey. I managed to put him into a sleeping trance to try and calm him, but he's still fighting it. If he can't break the Shadow spell, you'll be in danger.'

'Me?' said Dido. 'How come?'

Mum looked around the room, as though she didn't know what to say, but not before Dido had seen the fear in her eyes. 'The voice told him to kill you, Dido,' Mum said.

10
Changes

Scott propped himself up on his left elbow and listened intently. An unfamiliar sound had woken him up, and it took him a few seconds to realise what it was – silence. There was no noise of traffic from the street outside, no whistling, bottle-rattling milkman. The house was silent too. It was ominous.

Then Scott noticed the cold, and the hard white light shining through his bedroom curtains. He got up, grabbed his dressing gown from behind the door, hauled it on and went to the window. He drew back the curtain, and the unexpectedness of what he saw made him laugh aloud.

Springbrook Close had been transformed into a winter wonderland of thick drifts and sparkling crystals, with icicles hanging from the edges of every roof. Scott looked upwards, half expecting to see Santa and his reindeer sleigh sail across the sky. Quite a few people seemed to have entered into the spirit of the weather. They were outside their houses, heaping up snow to make snowmen.

'Hey, par-ty!' said Scott.

He couldn't believe how crazily people were acting, until he focused on the Metcalfe family directly opposite. Scott vaguely knew the Metcalfes' son, Dean, because he was a Prince Arthur's pupil, but Dean was in Year Eleven, and though they were neighbours, Scott and Dean had hardly ever spoken to each other. Dean and his mother were beavering away, and seemed normal enough to a casual glance, but closer observation revealed that they were moving oddly. Their actions were as stilted and frantic as the gestures of actors in a silent movie. Mr Metcalfe wasn't moving much, a sure sign that he was the one in charge. He was leaning on the handle of a spade, darting a finger here and there as he directed the proceedings. Scott could have sworn that Dean gave his father a snappy salute.

And what were they making?

Are those tentacles? thought Scott. *Snowmen don't have* tentacles!

Similar scenes were taking place in the rest of the street. People were scampering about like zombies on fast-forward. Apparently, no one had even noticed that Springbrook Close had changed too. The houses were taller and thinner. Gables seemed to have altered their positions, and there were two snow-covered shapes on the gateposts of number Twenty-Seven that hadn't been there before.

'Dido,' Scott muttered. 'This is definitely a Dido thing.'

He went to the bathroom, steeling himself for the customary morning wrangle with Kate, but for once the bathroom was empty.

'Cool!' Scott said to himself. 'But then it would be, with all that snow outside.'

Twenty minutes later, Scott was washed, dressed and ready to rock. He went downstairs, heading for the kitchen, figuring that since no one else was up yet, he might as well make tea for everybody and earn himself a few bonus points.

But he was wrong. His mother and sisters were standing in a line in front of the sink, apparently hypnotised by something they could see from the window. They were so quiet and still that Scott said, 'What's the big attraction?'

Mum, Kate and Julie slowly turned in unison.

They were each holding a kitchen knife, the blades shining in the snow-reflected sunlight.

In his downstairs bedsit on Abbey Street, near the town centre, John crouched over an antique single-bar electric fire, trying to stay warm as he munched at a bacon sandwich and listened to the radio. It was tuned in to Radio Stanstowe, a station that John didn't bother with as a rule. It was strictly for kids – all boy-bands and girl-bands, and more like pap music than pop music. This morning though, John was anxious to catch the local news and find out if the weather was going to improve or get worse.

'Here's an urgent traffic report,' said a cheery DJ, sounding as chirpy as a love-struck budgerigar. 'The County Council has hired six snowploughs from M4 maintenance depots, which should go into action later this morning, and the Army has offered troops from Ardfield and Dibshot to help with the clear-up. Meanwhile, local police and motoring organisations strongly advise drivers not to attempt to drive into or out of Stanstowe. But who wants to, when you can kick back, chill and listen to Radio Stanstowe, the station that plays the latest sounds around – like this, the new Number One from—'

A gloved hand appeared at the window, squeaking as it rubbed a circular patch free of frost.

John shot out of his chair, like ten thousand volts had been passed through it.

Bivco was outside on the street, beckoning to him. John groaned and went to open the door.

Bivco wore the same black outfit that John had last seen him in, except he'd added a long, black-leather overcoat that gave him a Nazi look. Bivco's pupils were tiny, and John wondered what he was on.

Bivco spread his arms wide and said, 'Told you! Didn't I tell you?'

'Did you?' said John.

'I told you there were going to be changes, and here they are.'

John sniffed. It was just a bit of snow. He didn't see what Bivco was making such a fuss about.

Then he looked around, and *saw*.

His bedsit *had* been part of a shabby Regency terrace, but the building was no longer recognisable. It had Gothic spires and intricate stone tracery that reminded John of a cathedral.

'Huh?' John said.

He stepped out of the doorway into the street, and looked up.

Something clung under the eaves, a stone animal of some kind. John made out a flattened, dog-like head with pointed ears, and a squat scaly body with a stubby tail.

'What's that, when it's at home?' said John.

'A gargoyle.'

'Wasn't there yesterday.'

Bivco shrugged.

'Is today,' he said. 'Changes, Johnno. Real changes. The potential in things is coming out.'

'You what?'

'Try and stay up to speed, Johnno. This town's turning into what it ought to be, what it used to be, years ago. The Shadow One's taking back what belongs to Him.'

John ran a hand through his hair. A lot of weirdness had happened to him over the last couple of days, and he didn't want to accept any of it.

'Get away!' he snorted. 'This is one of them whatsits, isn't it? A makeover, like they do on TV.'

Bivco shook his head sadly.

'Wise up, Johnno,' he said. 'Things aren't the same

any more. Grab a coat and come with me.'

'Where we going?'

'Exploring.'

John looked down and shuffled his feet in the snow.

'I don't know, Biv,' he said. 'Like, on the radio, the police said people shouldn't go out.'

'Look at me!' Bivco shouted.

John's head snapped up as if a string had pulled it. He and Bivco locked gazes. Purple sparks glowed deep in Bivco's eyes. The glow brightened and dimmed in a rhythmic pulse.

'We're going exploring,' Bivco said.

John couldn't look away. Bivco's eyes were brighter than Christmas lights.

'Sure, Biv,' John said. 'Anything you say, mate.'

Scott did exactly as he was told. He didn't have any choice. If he tried to put up a fight, it would be three against one, with the one unarmed and the three carrying knives. Something had got into his mother and sisters, and turned them into strangers. The envelopes looked the same, but the messages inside had been changed.

Shadow Magic, thought Scott.

He'd seen Shadow Magic at work in Year Seven, when a Shadowmaster's spell had left Philippa dangling in mid-air during a Drama lesson. Now it had invaded his home and was looking at him through the eyes of Kate and Julie. They held their knives pointed at his chest, while Mum used a length of plastic-coated washing line to tie him to one of the kitchen chairs.

'Hands behind your back,' said Mum.

Scott felt the line draw tight around his wrists.

Stay calm, he thought. Don't do anything to spook them.

Staying calm wasn't easy. Scott was in the most terrifying nightmare of his life, and it was really happening.

'There's no talking to you, is there, Scott?' Mum said. 'You swan around like you own this place. You never listen to what I say. You take me for granted – unless you want something. You're turning out just like your father – you're even starting to look like him.'

'Yes, Mum,' said Scott. 'Sorry, Mum.'

Mum crouched, took the line under the seat of the chair and began to bind Scott's ankles.

'You were always the favourite, Scott,' Kate said.

'It was great until you were born. I was Mum and Dad's little princess, then you came along and took them away from me. You got away with murder.'

'You think you can boss me around all the time, just because you're older than me,' said Julie.

In his detached state, Scott understood what the Shadow Magic was doing. It had taken all the little deep-seated family resentments and exaggerated them until they were out of all proportion. Dido had described Shadow Magic in terms of spectacular pyrotechnics and scary monsters, but Scott was learning that it could be far more subtle, and that the monsters were ordinary.

Mum tied off the last knot and stood upright.

'When are we going to do it, Mum?' asked Kate.

'Not just yet, love,' Mum said. 'We have to build a totem first.'

'What's a totem?' said Julie.

Mum smiled at her.

'We're going to make a dragon out of snow and give it things,' she explained. 'The first thing we're going to give it is Scott.'

Scott waited. It seemed to take hours for Mum, Kate and Julie to put on their coats in the hall, but at last he heard the front door close.

Scott knew a thing or two about ropes and knots. When he was younger, he'd had an ambition to be a stage conjuror and escape artist. He'd read loads of books, and spent hours practising with string, and plastic handcuffs. So, while Mum had tied him up, Scott had kept his muscles tensed. Now he relaxed, and the line wrapped around him slackened slightly. He flexed his fingers experimentally. It was almost a year since he'd done any tricks – what if he'd forgotten his old skills?

Don't go there! Scott thought. You're not Scott Pink, you're the Great Voodini, and you have to give the performance of a lifetime.

In his imagination, Scott saw himself on stage, in the centre of a spotlight. A drummer down in the orchestra pit struck up a long roll.

Scott's fingers picked and teased. He ignored the pain in his straining tendons, and the soreness of the washing line chafing his wrists. Mum wasn't an expert in knot-tying and, in theory, escaping ought to be easy.

'This is child's play to the Great Voodini!' Scott grunted.

His right hand slipped free. He released his left hand, pushed the loop of line around his chest up over his shoulders and leaned over to work on his ankles.

When Scott had untied himself, he didn't hang around. He unbolted the kitchen door and ran down the back garden as fast as he could through the snow. There was only one person who could help him, only one person that he was certain he could trust.

He had to find Dido.

11
Nearest and Dearest

Ollie had inherited second sight from his grandmother on his dad's side of the family. Granny Falkener had been a full-blown Light Witch, like Dido, and had trained him to develop his gift. Now he wished that she hadn't taught him anything, because what his second sight revealed was frightening.

The purple-grey dust he'd seen in Alder Drive was all over the garden, his parents and Steve. Their faces were caked in it, giving their skin an unhealthy, decomposing look – and they'd gone mad.

No, they're not mad, Ollie thought. They're being controlled by Shadow Magic.

He could just about catch the voice that his parents were obeying, but it was like trying to hear someone while listening to music on headphones, and he missed patches.

Ollie was playing a dangerous game, pretending that he was under control too. He'd worked on the snow dinosaur with his parents, copying the way they moved, pausing when they paused. It had worked so far, but Ollie was still planning to make a break for it when the right time came.

Mr Falkener said, 'He is pleased.'

'We have served him well,' said Mrs Falkener.

'Praised be his name,' Steve said.

There was an expectant pause.

In the same flat tone that Steve had used, Ollie said, 'Praised be his name.'

The Tyrannosaurus Rex was almost finished. The most difficult part had been making the shortened forelimbs, which had kept falling off. Ollie had come up with the answer by suggesting that they use two potting-forks from the garden shed. The dinosaur's tail had been moulded round a hosepipe, and wooden clothes pegs had been slotted into its jaws as teeth.

The voice spoke again. Ollie concentrated hard.

'*...warned ... your son ... not all he seems ... enemies must be eliminated ...*'

Uh oh! thought Ollie. I've been rumbled.

Ollie's parents and brother gazed at him

with dust-clotted eyes.

'I'm going inside,' Ollie said.

'For what reason, Oliver?' asked Mr Falkener.

'Call of nature.'

'Very well, but don't be long. We have an urgent matter to discuss.'

When he turned the corner of the house, out of his parents' sight, Ollie flattened himself against the wall and listened.

'It seems that Oliver has deceived us,' he heard his father say. 'He is disloyal and headstrong.'

'We should punish him,' Steve said.

Ollie's fear went up a notch, and he started to shake.

Mr Falkener said, 'What punishment would be suitable, d'you think?'

That did it for Ollie. He scrambled down the side of the house and set off down the road.

Dido's inseeing showed the spell horribly clearly. It was like a broad hand with an eye in the knuckle of every finger and a mouth in the thumb. The fingers were gripping the top of her father's skull and the nails were sunk into his scalp. Aware that Dido could see it, the hand clenched its fingers more tightly and Dad groaned in his sleep.

Dido wanted to scream, and throw up.

How dare it! she thought. How dare it come into our home!

The spell caught the thought.

'I dare anything, Light Witch,' said the thumb-mouth.

'Mum,' Dido said quietly. 'Can you see it?'

'Not distinctly,' Mum said. 'It's very fuzzy. It must be blocking my inseeing somehow. What is it?'

'Haven't the faintest, but it's sapping Dad's strength. His aura's getting faint.'

Cosmo, crouched at Dido's feet, puffed herself up and hissed venomously.

'Yeah, I wish it would too, Coz,' said Dido, 'but I don't think it's got the biological equipment.'

The spell grew anxious. It swivelled its eyes from Dido, to Mum, to Cosmo and back again.

Dido knew that she had to do something soon. Dad's aura told her that he couldn't hold out much longer.

'Move away from the sofa, Mum,' said Dido. 'Lullaby.'

'You want me to sing a—'

'Just do it!'

Mum's voice was hesitant at first, but as the song worked its magic, it soothed her, and her voice strengthened.

Cosmo's fur went flat, and her eyelids drooped.

The spell detested the lullaby. It gnashed its teeth and all its eyes turned on Mum, certain that she was about to launch an attack.

A spell burst out of Dido, stinging like a scab peeling off a wound that hadn't fully healed.

The pattern at the far edge of the lounge rug twitched. The reds, blues and creams ran together in a grey stream that climbed the arm of the sofa, behind Dad's head. The stream turned solid and put out tendrils that sprouted sharp dark thorns. The tendrils reared, then dropped on to the hand-thing, twining around the fingers, piercing the eyes with their thorns, thrusting their way into the mouth, growing through the body of the spell and bursting out.

The spell's skin wrinkled, melted into slime, into mist, into nothing.

The tendrils ebbed back into the rug.

Cosmo looked up at Dido and purred.

'Thanks,' said Dido. 'But stop calling me *kid*, will you?'

Mum stepped over to Dad and stroked his face. His eyes opened and he grimaced.

'Have two teams of hippos been playing a game of rugby in my head?' he said, and Mum burst into tears.

Dido and Cosmo tactfully withdrew from the lounge, to let Mum and Dad have some quality time.

Over breakfast, Dad described what had happened when he'd inseen the snow werewolf in Charlie Morrison's garden.

'I lost myself,' he said. 'I know I wasn't talking or behaving rationally, but there was nothing I could do. When I used my magic, it made the Shadow spell stronger. It's not an experience I'd care to repeat in a hurry.'

'It hasn't spoiled your appetite though,' said Mum. 'That's your fourth piece of toast.'

'I'm a growing boy,' said Dad. He looked enquiringly at Dido. 'That's your thinking face, isn't it?'

'No, it's my puzzled face,' said Dido. 'Shadow Magic got to you and Mr Morrison, but not me or Mum. Why didn't we all fall under the spell?'

'Because Spelkor brings chaos,' said Dad. 'That's what the snow statues are all about. Spelkor is making people build creatures that give shape to their deepest fears. It's a sign of his power. Anyone who doesn't build a statue will be seen as an enemy. Spelkor sets families against one another, friend against friend. It's completely random – it wouldn't be chaos otherwise, would it?'

Dad's mention of family and friends reminded Dido that Lilil had told her to watch over those who were near to her, and she wondered how Ollie, Scott and Philippa were. Before the thought had finished crossing Dido's mind, her magic took charge of her inseeing and split her in two.

It was bizarre. One Dido was still at the breakfast table with Mum and Dad, while the other Dido hung in the sky, high above Stanstowe. This Dido was part condor, part aeroplane, made of black feathers and metal plates. Her outstretched wings adjusted themselves to hold her position in the shifting air current. She was a wind-rider, free to go anywhere. In her world, there were no walls or boundaries.

This is brilliant! Dido thought, and whooped for joy, but the whoop emerged as a dry croak that was harsher than cinders.

Dido looked down and saw through magic.

Stanstowe was a battlefield, lit by ripples of purple flashes like exploding artillery shells. Her sharp condor eyes allowed her to see in minute detail. She could make out the faces of the people who were out on the streets, and the faces of the snow statues they were sculpting – demons, vampires, ghouls. All over town, the half-forgotten creatures of childhood nightmares were taking shape.

Dido's vision and will fused. She thought of Ollie and saw him walking along Stanstowe Road, following the path cleared by a snow plough that was trundling towards the town centre. Ollie, Dido knew, was heading for her house. So was Scott, who was floundering through the drifts on Barleycorn Drive, three streets away from where she lived.

And Philippa? Although in her present form Dido didn't have thumbs, she felt them itching anyway. She folded her wings and went into a dive.

The streets rushed up at her, expanding as she descended. Dido fixed on Hazelwood Close, levelled out at the last minute and flew straight through Philippa's front door, along the hallway, into the kitchen, out and up into the air again. She was in the house for less than a second, but that had been more than enough for her to sense the power that was at work there.

The two Didos reunited with a shock that clicked her teeth together.

Mum said, 'Have you been—?'

'Inseeing, yes,' said Dido, standing up. 'I must ring Philippa.'

She went into the hall and dialled Philippa's mobile number. Philippa answered at once.

'Oh, hi, Dido. I was just about to call you.'

'Where are you?' Dido said.

'In my bedroom, listening to my stereo.'

'And Tom?'

'In his bedroom. We're keeping clear of Dad and Alison. They've been—'

'I know,' said Dido. 'Are they downstairs?'

'No. They're doing something in the back garden – goodness knows what.'

'You and Tom have got to get out of the house. Don't let your dad or Alison see you. Come over to my place.'

'But—'

'No time.'

'What?'

'No time for that either. Go!'

Philippa hung up.

Dido listened to the hum of the disengaged tone and prayed that she hadn't left it too late.

12
Obstacles

Scott was hurting. He'd taken off without a coat, or gloves, or breakfast, and now he was paying the price. His hands were blue and his fingers throbbed, the pain making them feel huge. His feet were like chunks of wood, so every step was an effort that was accompanied by the loud gurgling of his stomach. He needed to rest and eat something in a warm place, but there was only snow and more snow.

Come on! Scott urged himself. Move your legs. That's a metre closer to Dido's house, and another, and another ...

Reality shifted. A combination of shock, hunger and exhaustion made Scott start to hallucinate – or he *hoped* that he was hallucinating.

There were faces in the trunks of the trees on Barleycorn Drive. Their hollow eyes stared at him from below their hair-branches. A snowbound car at the side of the road leered with its radiator-grin. The alien giraffes of the street lamps bent their necks to inspect him.

'*You are alone*,' said a voice.

'Oh, terrific!' Scott said. 'Now I'm hearing things.'

'*Alone is one*.'

'Yeah, yeah. Keep talking.'

'*One has no power. One leaves things unchanged. One can make no difference. One times one is one, one times two is two, one times three is three*—'

'You've made your point,' said Scott. 'If this is me I'm talking to, could we change the subject?'

He drew level with a garden in which an elderly couple were sculpting a sea serpent whose head was raised above the billows of snow-waves.

The sea serpent hissed at him.

'*I know where you are going*,' it said. '*You think you will be safe there? You think that she will protect you – but why should she?*'

'Because I'm her friend,' said Scott.

The sea serpent laughed scornfully.

'*Her friend?*' it sneered. '*You are a pet, a plaything to her. She toys with you when the mood takes her, but her real feelings, her deep true feelings, belong to another*.'

Scott felt a hurt that was keener than the cold.

'I know,' he said. 'I'm not an idiot.'

'They laugh at you in secret. They call you her puppy.'

'No they don't!'

'Are you sure of that?'

Scott didn't reply. He concentrated on getting past the garden.

'You can turn your back and walk away,' said the sea serpent, *'but you will carry the truth of my words with you.'*

At the corner of Barleycorn Drive, a pillar box inclined its domed top and the edges of its slot softened into lips.

'Turn back! Your mother and your sisters need you. They do not know what they are doing, but you can set them right.'

Anger flashed through Scott.

'And what would you know about it?' he growled. 'What d'you know about families, friends or anything? Stop wasting my time. Go play blind man's buff on the M4.'

The pillar box stiffened into cast-iron silence and the street resumed normality.

Scott sensed that he'd overcome an obstacle, but forgetting what the voice had told him wasn't going to be so easy.

Does Dido really treat me like a pet? he thought.

He searched his memories as the seed of doubt that the voice had planted took root.

Ollie made steady progress along the newly cleared road. He'd never actually walked to Dido's house before, but he knew the way. When he reached the bus stop where Dido and Scott caught the bus to school, he turned right into Poppy Street. Halfway down the street, Ollie came to a halt.

Poppy Street seemed to have altered. Though most of the houses were hidden by snow, the bits that showed were unfamiliar. Ollie didn't recall any dragon finials on the roofs, or latticed windows, or stone porches carved with five-pointed stars when he'd last been there.

Did I get the right bus stop? Ollie wondered.

He pushed on to the road sign at the end of the street and cleared the snow from it – Witchgallows Street.

Puzzled, Ollie turned the corner.

According to the sign, the next street was Nighthag Drive, which was free of snow, in a different climate and a different time. The houses had wattle-and-daub walls and heavy black beams.

They were crowded together: the rooftops on either side of the cobbled road leaned over so far that they almost touched.

Ollie's common sense told him to go back to Stanstowe Road, but he wasn't in a commonsense situation. Shadow Magic pulled at him.

I'm wimping out, Ollie said to himself. I'm running to Dido so she can rescue me.

Ever since he'd known Dido, Ollie had been in awe of her powers. They made his second sight look pathetic, like a consolation prize. This was a chance to prove himself, to show Dido that he could stand up to Shadow Magic just as well as she could.

This is a challenge, Ollie thought. I can either go back and forget about going to Dido's house, or I can try and find my way through whatever Shadow Magic throws at me.

He squared his shoulders, took a step forwards and let second sight lead him on.

Ollie crossed into Nighthag Drive, his confidence growing with every step. It wasn't so bad. No freaky faces peeked at him from the darkened windows, no bolts of lightning crackled down from the sky to zap him.

Nighthag Drive joined Succubus Lane at a T-junction, and the houses changed yet again. A row of pretty thatched cottages stood beside a rough track that was scarred with deep ruts. Purple roses were in bloom around the doorways and the heavy sweetness of their scent made Ollie's head swim.

A plump woman came out of one of the cottages and beckoned to Ollie.

Cautiously he approached her.

She was tiny, nearly as round as she was tall. Her eyes were brown and her cheeks were red. Her broad forehead and turned-up nose made her look more like a giant baby than a woman. She smiled, revealing discoloured teeth.

'I knew you'd pass by this way sooner or later, m'dear,' she said.

'That's more than I did,' said Ollie.

The woman laughed wheezily.

'That's because I'm wise, m'dear,' she said. 'I know what's what, and I know what's what with you.'

'Really?' Ollie said sarcastically.

'You're moonstruck and lovelorn. The one you dream of dreams of someone else, and that makes for heartache.'

Ollie was taken aback. The strange little woman had seen straight through him.

'Her name starts with a P,' the woman said. 'P for pretty and P for pitiless. His name starts with an S. S for stubborn and S for sly. If only she could see him for what he is, and you for what you are, eh?' She came closer and lowered her voice. 'And that's where I can help you, m'dear.'

'You can?'

The woman nodded vigorously and held up a glass vial, no bigger than her little finger. The vial was filled with a clear, violet liquid and stoppered with a minute cork.

'Slip this into her food or drink, doesn't matter which,' the woman said. 'Three drops for liking, six for a friend, nine for a true love that never will end.'

'Is it a love potion?' said Ollie.

'Not a potion, a philtre, m'dear. Coney-catchers brew potions for those with shallow wits and deep pockets, but I don't want paying. I just want to give a handsome young lad a helping hand.'

Ollie began to reach for the vial, but before he could take it his arm dropped to his side.

'No,' he said. 'It would be a lie.'

'Oh, what's a little lie between friends, m'dear?' cajoled the woman.

Ollie moved away.

'Who are you?' he demanded. 'How do I know you're not offering me poison?'

The woman's smile shrank into a scowl.

'You'll regret spurning my gift one day!' she spat.

There was a noise like tearing silk. Spiked green leaves grew out of the woman's face and her round body twisted and diminished.

Ollie was staring at a snow-choked holly bush in the front garden of a house in Bramble Way, and he felt like a complete idiot.

Tom was quiet as he and Philippa walked up Stanstowe Road, but Philippa knew that he was probably as scared as she was. Weirdness was everywhere. Dad and Alison weren't the only ones who'd made snow sculptures. Every other house they'd passed had a figure in the garden, and some of the figures were hideous.

The heavy responsibility of taking care of Tom gave Philippa an attack of the Big Sisters.

'It'll be all right, Tom,' she said. 'The weather's been peculiar and it's made people peculiar too.'

'They're not peculiar, they're loopy!' Tom snorted. 'Why are we going to Dido's?'

'Because she'll explain what's happening.'

'How can anyone explain this lot?'

Philippa selected her words carefully.

'Dido's clever,' she said. 'She has...special talents.'

'What kind of talents?'

The sound of a vehicle made Tom and Philippa turn their heads.

A police car was coming up behind them. The car slowed, pulled alongside and the driver's window slid down.

The driver was a police sergeant, with a square face and close-cropped grey hair.

'What the blazes are you kids up to?' he rasped.

'We're on our way to a friend's house,' said Philippa.

'Whereabouts?'

'Mistletoe Lane.'

The sergeant scowled.

'Haven't you heard the news on Radio Stanstowe? It's not safe. There are some funny people about,' he said. He leaned over the back of his seat and opened the passenger door. 'You'd better come with us.'

Philippa felt relieved. Someone else was going to

take care of her and Tom.

'You first, Tom,' she said.

Tom looked uncertain.

'I thought we weren't supposed to take lifts from strangers,' he said.

'Don't be stupid!' Philippa said. 'Policemen aren't strangers.'

Tom got into the car and Philippa followed. The sergeant activated the central-locking system and the car edged forwards at walking pace.

There was a police constable in the front passenger's seat. He was younger than the sergeant. His pale face was expressionless, but his eyes darted anxiously from side to side.

'Where are we going, Sarge?' he asked.

'Never you mind,' said the sergeant. 'These two may be able to assist us with our enquiries. I'll do the talking, you take the notes – got it?'

'Yes, Sarge.'

The sergeant glanced at Philippa's reflection in the rear-view mirror.

'What's your totem, Miss?' he said.

'My what?' Philippa gasped.

'My colleague and I are followers of the Bearded Head. The Shadow One has many forms. How did he reveal himself to you?'

'I'm sorry,' said Philippa, 'I don't—'

She broke off as Tom dug her in the ribs with his elbow.

'We built a centaur in our garden,' Tom told the sergeant.

'Oh?'

'It's massive. It took us ages. We call it Chiron.'

The sergeant cocked his head to one side as though listening to something, then smiled grimly.

'You're lying,' he said. 'I'm taking you both to Stanstowe Police Station for further interrogation.'

The constable squirmed.

'Hang on, Sarge!' he said. 'Aren't they a bit young to—'

'Don't let their age fool you, constable,' the sergeant interrupted. 'They're associates of the enemy. Can't you smell it?'

'What are you going to do with us?' Philippa said hesitantly.

'Put you in a place where you can't make any mischief. You'll be dealt with later, when it's over.'

'When what's over?'

'Everything,' said the sergeant.

Philippa's world went into slow motion. A black

dog careened out into the road, its eyes and teeth flashing as it barked furiously. The sergeant's body stiffened. His right foot slammed down on the brake pedal while his hands spun the steering wheel over to the left. The rear of the car slewed and the vehicle went into a skid, its tyres squealing thinly. A snow-covered car loomed up in the windscreen, and then the windscreen burst into glittering crumbs. The jolt of the impact smacked the sergeant's head against the pillar of the driver's door. He groaned and slumped forwards, stunned.

With a single, well-practised movement, the young constable produced a pair of handcuffs from his belt and fastened the sergeant's wrists to the steering wheel. He looked over his shoulder at Philippa and Tom.

'You OK?' he said.

'I think so,' said Philippa, staring at the sergeant. 'What's wrong with him?'

'Your guess is as good as mine,' said the constable. 'I've been stringing them along all morning.'

'Them?'

'Half the town's like it, including the local police. I've had it. I'm getting out of here, and I advise you to do the same. Get to your friend's house as fast as you can, and if you meet any police on the way, don't trust them. Don't trust anybody.'

'Let's go, sis!' said Tom.

Philippa was paralysed with panic.

'I can't!' she wailed. 'If I get out of the car, something awful will happen.'

'It already has,' Tom said grimly. 'Now move your butt!'

13
Temple of Shadows

John had lived in Stanstowe all his life, but not the Stanstowe that Bivco led him through. The layout of the streets was more or less the same, but the roads were narrower and more crooked, the houses mean and cramped. For a while John managed to convince himself that he was in a bad dream and would wake up soon, but reality struck him as he stepped over a gutter that was choked with steaming filth. The stench made his eyes water. He covered his mouth with his hand and coughed.

'We going much further, Biv?' he enquired. 'Only the stink round here makes me want to puke.'

Bivco took in a deep breath through his nose, and let it out with an appreciative sigh.

'That's the true smell of humanity, Johnno,' he said. 'People don't like to be reminded of it.

They cover it up with deodorants and perfume.'

'Can't say I blame them.'

Bivco squared his shoulders.

'People have gone soft,' he said. 'They live in the same kind of houses, eat the same packaged food, watch the same TV programmes. Then they get into their cars and drive to other towns that are identical to the ones they've left. It's all wrong, Johnno. It's too easy. There has to be struggle, so that the strong can take over from the weak. The human race is going to be purified, and the purification starts here.'

John's forehead creased into a troubled frown.

'Steady on, Biv!' he said. 'That's a bit racist, isn't it?'

'Racism doesn't come into it, Johnno.' Bivco thumped himself on the chest. 'It's what's in here that counts. You're either with us or against us, and if you're against us, you're the enemy.'

'Who are we, Biv?'

'Hey?'

'You said that if you're not with us, you're against us, yeah? I was wondering who *we* were.'

Bivco looked surprised.

'We're the servants of the Shadow One,' he said. 'We've been his servants for years.'

'We have?'

'Remember that deputy head we had when we were in school – Old Ma Baker? She was down on us all the time, wasn't she?'

'Right old cow!' John said.

'But we fixed her good and proper, didn't we, Johnno? We took that squirrel and—'

'Yeah,' John said quickly. 'I remember.'

A vivid snatch of long-supressed memory came back to him: twigs popping in a fire at the centre of the Speaking Stones, smoke gusting up into the night; the shrieking of the squirrel; the wet redness on his hands. And then words had filled his mind, words from nowhere, words he didn't know the meaning of. He and Bivco had started chanting simultaneously.

Palecorum alneth la,
Saletarum detha na,
Vida nectus,
Kalam si,
Talla mectus ifte da.

'That was Him,' said Bivco. 'His spirit was in us that night. He taught us what to do and what to say. He chose us. It was His power that sent Old Ma Baker round the twist.'

They turned a corner, and John thought that he must have gone round the twist too.

Dead ahead, where the Pentacle shopping mall should have been, stood an immense building of black stone, bristling with towers, and spires that rose to points that looked sharper than syringes. Gargoyles leered down from the towers, and there were statues of hooded figures set in niches in the walls. Some of the figures held swords and flails, others held scythes and hourglasses. At the apex of the great domed roof, a five-pointed star made of tempered metal gave off a violet glow.

John gulped.

'What's that then, Biv?' he whispered.

'The Temple of Shadows,' said Bivco. 'Come on.'

He took a step towards the building.

John's jaw dropped.

'We're not going inside, are we?' he said, his voice rising to a dry squeak.

'We certainly are,' Bivco said cheerfully. 'Where else would we go?'

The entrance to the temple had been shaped into the gaping mouth of a gigantic serpent with stalactite fangs that dripped water on to the threshold. The interior was bizarrely sumptuous, with a floor of lilac-grey marble slabs, inlaid with a mosaic of interlocking purple pentagrams. Thick fluted pillars rose up, their tops branching into stone fountains that supported the roof.

Light streamed in through stained-glass windows that depicted scenes from fairy tales. John thought he recognised some of them, but they seemed to be illustrating parts of the stories that he hadn't read: a dragon devouring a knight in silver armour; a cruel-faced queen surrounded by dead dwarves, holding aloft a human heart, blood running down her arms and staining the sleeves of her gown; a gore-muzzled wolf wearing a red hooded cape, standing on its hind legs in the doorway of a cottage.

In the middle of the temple was an altar, a rough block of weather-beaten stone. Bivco strode up to it, and traced his fingers along the shallow grooves that had been carved into its upper surface.

'This is where we'll sacrifice the Shadow One's enemies,' he said.

'Sacrifice?' said John, blinking hard.

Bivco nodded.

John did some rapid calculation. There was no way

he'd come out on top if he took Bivco on in a fight, but if he ran fast enough—

Bivco smiled tenderly.

'Don't even think about it, Johnno,' he said. 'You wouldn't get as far as the door – look.'

John turned his head, and saw people streaming into the temple.

'Well all right!' crowed Bivco. 'Let's get ready for show time!'

Jack, Ross and David sculpted their toad-wolverine in the park, next to the statue of Ezra Hunter. They had a great laugh, giggling away like they were high on something. Jack was hazy about how the Terrible Trio had wound up in the park. When he tried to remember, the big warm voice spoke in his head, and then nothing else mattered.

'I am well pleased in you, my boy. You have hit it off just so. No one else could make it as perfectly as you.'

Jack was rapt. He and the voice were on the same wavelength – he understood precisely what it wanted him to do, and he got a big kick out of doing it.

When the statue was complete, the three boys gazed at it in awe.

'Terrific, isn't it?' said Ross. 'Really terrific. I mean, it's sort of like—'

'Terrific,' David said. 'What d'you reckon made us think of it, Jack?'

'Shut it, will you?' Jack said tersely. 'I'm getting a message.'

Ross and David exchanged glances. Jack had been like it all morning, acting as if he were talking to someone on the phone, only there was no phone.

Jack said, 'Yeah. Yeah. What – now? Sure. No worries. Sorted.' He looked at his mates. 'OK, lads, we're going into town.'

David wasn't too keen on the idea.

'What, through all the snow and that?' he gasped.

'Yes,' said Jack, mimicking his tone, 'through all the snow and that.'

'What for?'

'Because I've been told to, you big dipstick.'

'Who by?'

Jack narrowed his eyes.

'What's the matter, Dave, lost your bottle?' he said. 'You'd better make your mind up fast, pal. Are you with us, or against us?'

Jack had always been the leader of the three because he was the quickest-witted, but now there was something else about him, a menace that warned David he would be dangerous to cross.

'With you, of course,' David said. 'No question, Jack.'

Jack relaxed.

'Good,' he said. 'So let's get going. Don't want to miss all the fun, do we?'

'What fun's that, Jack?' asked Ross.

'All the fun of the fair,' Jack said with a grin.

It took more than two hours for the temple to fill. Bivco had been right, racism had nothing to to with it – every ethnic group in Stanstowe was represented in the congregation, though John noticed that everybody had the same expression, with eyes as glassy and vacant as empty greenhouses.

Bivco stood in front of the altar, his arms folded across his chest.

'Welcome, all!' he said, his voice echoing off the walls. 'We have been drawn here by the Shadow One.'

'The Shadow One!' the crowd repeated.

'The Time of the Stars is upon us,' Bivco went on. 'At midnight, He will rise from His prison and walk among us. His strength will be our strength, and our strength will be His. We will be the instruments of His wrath, bringing despair and death to His enemies. No one will be spared, not the highest or the lowest, not your children or your parents. There are no families any more, no friendships, no loyalties above the loyalty we owe to Him. Serve Him faithfully and do what I say.'

'Who made you our leader?' called out someone in the crowd. 'How can we be sure that you speak for the Shadow One?'

Other voices shouted back, and for a moment the temple was filled with an anger and confusion that threatened to boil over into violence.

Bivco slowly unfolded his arms, and held out his hands.

'Behold!' he cried.

Purple light beamed out of his eyes and cast slanting shadows across the marble floor.

Silence fell. The crowd dropped to its knees.

John knelt like the others, but then his nerve broke. He lay on his side, drew his knees up to his chest, wrapped his arms around them to make himself into a ball, and whimpered like a terrified puppy.

14
Invitation for Nine

Scott was the first to reach Dido's house; Ollie, Philippa and Tom arrived shortly after. Mum charged around, finding dry clothes and clean towels. Dad cooked a pile of bacon and scrambled eggs. Once spare chairs had been brought down from upstairs, everybody sat round the table and tucked in.

While she ate, Dido checked out her friends with inseeing. According to the colours in their auras, they'd all taken a knock. Ollie's aura was suffused with pink, indicating that he'd done something that he wasn't proud of. The hint of grey in the light surrounding Philippa suggested that her confidence had been shaken. Tom was enclosed in a confused white fog. The toughest aura to read was Scott's, it had a murky green tinge that might mean jealousy, or something more serious.

Dido broke contact and thought, They're all

hiding stuff that would be better in the open.

Mum must have come to the same conclusion, because she said, 'Did you and Tom have any trouble getting here, Philippa?'

Dido admired Mum's choice. It didn't take much to get Philippa talking.

Philippa embarked on a detailed account of her and Tom's experiences with the patrol car.

'It was awful!' she concluded. 'Just when I thought we were safe, we were most in danger.'

'That's Shadow Magic for you,' said Mum. 'It can be really sneaky. How about you, Ollie?'

'I was conned,' Ollie said. 'I got suckered into using my second sight, and it made me cocky. I thought I could handle anything that was thrown at me. Then it tried to tempt me.'

'How?'

'Oh, it offered me a magic thing,' Ollie said airily.

Twigging that this was important, Dido said, 'What sort of magic thing?'

'It doesn't really matter.'

'Yes it does,' said Dido. 'We have to be totally straight. If we hold things back it's like lying, and when friends lie to each other, it makes Shadow Magic stronger.'

'It was a potion to make people like me,' Ollie said.

'But people do like you!'

Ollie's face burned red.

'Special kind of liking,' he mumbled.

'Did you take it?' Dido demanded.

Ollie looked straight at her, embarrassed and offended.

'Of course not!' he said.

Everyone turned to Scott, who avoided eye contact by staring at the table. His hands were clenched into fists.

'I saw things,' he said. 'They talked to me. They told me that that Dido likes Ollie more than me, and that people joke about it.'

'It's not true!' exclaimed Dido.

Scott raised his eyes and peered at Dido through his fringe.

'Which part?' he said.

'Ollie and I do *not* joke about you.'

'But you do like him more than you like me.'

Now it was Dido's turn to blush.

'I like you both the same, but in different ways,' she said.

Scott was relentless.

'Sure,' he said. 'You like Ollie the way that I like

you, the way that Philippa likes me, the way that Ollie likes her.'

The atmosphere in the dining room was electric. Dido couldn't think of anything to say, and then, unbidden, her inseeing took charge.

Dido saw herself, Scott, Ollie and Philippa whirling round like a Catherine wheel, going faster and faster but never getting anywhere, just coming back to the same place, sooner with every spin. At the centre of the wheel was a stillness, and Dido's inseeing drew her inside where it was calm, and there was time to find words.

She said, 'You're right, Scott. I don't know whether teen hormones or Shadow Magic got us into this mess, but it's tearing us apart. We all want something more. We've been thinking about what we can't have so much, we've forgotten what's there. We're friends. Friendship is all we have to offer one another, and right now I need you guys.'

The wheel stopped spinning. Scott's, Ollie's and Philippa's auras cleared, and the electricity earthed itself.

'Ouch!' said Philippa. 'Why don't you tell it like it is, Dido?'

Ollie said, 'I've been a bit of a jerk, haven't I?'

'Not compared with me, you haven't,' said Scott.

Tom slammed down his knife and fork.

'What are you all on about?' he wailed. 'What's Shadow Magic?'

Dad explained, keeping it short and simple. 'Something nasty's happening in Stanstowe,' he said, 'and Dido's going to stop it.'

'How?'

'Good question,' said Dido. 'I'm supposed to sacrifice something, but I don't know what it is.'

'If you don't know what it is,' Tom said, 'how can you sacrifice it?'

'Beats me,' said Dido. 'I'm hoping for inspiration when the time comes.'

She heard the voice of the crone in her mind.

'Closer than blood and bone,
Hungry as fire,
Dearer than all you own,
Strong as desire,
Where strength and weakness are the same,
There love is hate, and loss is gain.'

What with one thing and another, Dido hadn't had any time to mull the verse over. It had to mean something – but what?

What's closer than blood and bone? Dido thought. How can strength and weakness be the same? Where does love become hate?

Her concentration was broken by the ringing of the doorbell. Dad went to answer it, and came back a few moments later with Miss Morgan.

Miss Morgan was stressed-out. Her voice quavered as she said, 'I hope I'm not interrupting anything, but I've had a most peculiar morning. It took me ages to get here. The main roads have been cleared, but there must be an emergency one-way system in operation. None of the traffic lights I went through brought me out where I wanted to go.'

'It's the Time of the Stars,' said Mum.

Miss Morgan's face paled.

'Oh!' she said. 'Isn't that when—' her eyes met Dido's, and she said, 'Oh!' again.

'Fascinating,' said Dad. 'The Shadow One attempted to mislead everybody on their way here, not just the people with power. It's as if he didn't want us to be together.'

Dido frowned, knowing that she was missing

something obvious.

'Why not?' said Ollie. 'Miss Morgan might be able to help Dido, but what use would Philippa, Tom, Scott and I be?'

The answer came to Dido in a sudden rush.

'There are nine of us,' she said.

'Of course!' said Mum.

Dad did a quick headcount and said, 'I only make it eight.'

Cosmo yowled indignantly from beneath Dido's chair.

Dad winced.

'Oops, sorry, Cosmo!' he said. 'Nine it is.'

'Nine?' said Philippa, mystified.

Mum had a teacher attack.

'All numbers have a magic significance, and three is especially important,' she said. 'It represents creativity and spiritual growth.'

'It's not only important in magic,' Dido added. 'Have you ever noticed how things happen three times in jokes? The punch line always comes the third time. There's also morning, noon and night, past, present and future, birth, life and death. All threes.'

'And nine is three multiplied by itself,' said Dad.

'We're far stronger together than we would be apart. It might help give you a fighting chance, Dido.'

'One can make no difference,' Scott said softly, remembering the voice he'd heard on Barleycorn Drive.

Dido's thumbs itched. She heard a distant whine that grew louder, and sensed an approaching darkness.

'Shielding spell!' she snapped.

Her magic was joined by her parents' magic, and a fraction of a second later, Miss Morgan's. A bubble of light swelled up over the table, its surface shimmering with iridescent colours that swirled.

The dining-room window disappeared behind a flat grey oblong.

There was a sound of whirring cogwheels. The grey oblong twitched. Wobbling numerals appeared on it, counting down from ten, and the room filled with tinny, wavering music. An image flashed up on the oblong: a group of people clinging to the side of a mountain, screaming in horror as a towering wave bore down on them.

A deep voice boomed out, 'Excitement as never before, thrills as never before!'

The picture changed. An avalanche engulfed a

pretty Alpine village; the spire of a church shattered.

'Spectacle as never before!' said the voice.

The cone of a volcano spouted a pillar of fire and smoke. City buildings collapsed as the earth shook and split. Panicking crowds were crushed under piles of falling rubble.

'Breathtaking scenes of wanton destruction!' the voice said. 'Innocence slaughtered!'

Desperate passengers hurled themselves from the deck of a sinking ship. Tanks smashed through walls. A road packed with refugees was strafed by a howling jet-fighter.

The music rose to a crescendo. The voice said, 'You are cordially invited to the premiere of The End of the World as You Know It. Tonight, at midnight, on Stanstowe Hill – one performance only!'

The oblong vanished as the protective bubble winked out.

'What was *that*?' said Scott.

'What it said it was, an invitation,' Dido said. 'Spelkor wants us to go to the Speaking Stones at midnight.'

'Why the rubbish movie trailer?'

'He's playing with us, trying to make himself seem less dangerous than he actually is.'

Philippa shuddered.

'But we're not falling for it, are we?' she said. 'It's obviously a trap.'

'Unless it's a double bluff,' said Dido. 'Like he's issued an invitation because he doesn't want us to come.'

'Is he that devious?'

Dido laughed bitterly.

'He's as devious as it gets, and then some,' she said.

'He's insecure too,' said Scott.

'Are you kidding – with *his* power?'

Scott shrugged.

'I don't know much about your kind of magic, Dido,' he said, 'but I know a cheap conjuring trick when I see one. Spelkor's scared.'

'Why would he be scared?'

'Because there are nine of us, but only one of him,' said Scott. 'He's alone.'

15
Voices in the Night

As night fell, the star on the dome of the temple shone more brightly, casting crooked shadows on to the uncleared snow, its purple light blending with the orange of the street lamps to make a colour without a name. No cars or pedestrians moved along the roads. Those unaffected by Shadow Magic were too afraid to leave their houses. They drew their curtains and locked their doors. Communication systems failed. Phone lines went dead. Television reception became so poor that the fuzzy pictures on the screens were unidentifiable. Radio stations were nothing but a blur of white noise.

Stanstowe was cut off from the outside world, a town besieged by itself.

A hush lay over the inside of the temple. Bivco had led a chant that lasted for more than an hour and tipped over into timelessness as, one by one, the followers of the Dark One fell into a trance. No one moved.

Or almost no one.

At the back of the congregation, in the shadows near the door, John crawled over the floor, using his arms to drag himself along, inching his way towards escape. At one point, considering how far gone everybody seemed, John had considered standing up and simply walking out – but didn't have the courage. Bivco – or whatever was using Bivco – might notice, and John didn't fancy being the first person to try out the altar. His plan was simple: he was going to sneak out of the temple, walk away and keep on walking until he reached a place where people were sane.

He was nearly there. He could see the iron jamb that raised the door's latch. In his mind he could already feel the cold metal under his thumb. Would it make a noise? Would the hinges creak? John prayed not.

He gathered himself into a crouch, reached out and—

'You all right?'

The whisper sounded louder than a shout.

John bit his lips to keep from crying out. It was

over; he'd been rumbled. With a hammering heart, he turned to see who'd spoken.

Two teenage boys peered at him. One was tall and beefy with a faceful of zits, the other was runty and spiky-haired.

John broke into a sweat.

'Fine!' he gabbled. 'Just a bit – I need a breath of fresh air, that's all. No one'll mind if I go outside for a minute, will they? I mean, I won't miss anything, will I? There's no need to—'

All of a sudden it registered that there was something different about the boys. Unlike the rest of the congregation, their eyes were clear and anxious, with sparks of life in them.

'Hang on a minute!' said John. 'You're not with *them*, are you?'

'Nah!' said the runt. 'We came with our mate Jack. He made us.'

Zit Face said, 'He's gone a bit ...' He crossed his eyes and circled an index finger in the air next to the side of his head.

'Reckon they all have, bar us,' said John, thinking, Great! Insurance! If they jump the three of us, one might be able to get away – preferably me. He leaned in closer to the boys and said, 'Want out, lads?'

'Too right!' said the runt. 'We've been thinking about it for a while now, but we didn't want to, like, be the first to leave, in case anybody lost their rag with us.'

John took charge.

'OK, stick with me,' he said. He looked at Zit Face. 'You look a bit handy, mate. Watch our backs for us, will you? If someone tries to stop us, take them out.'

He looked at the runt. 'You can give me a hand with the door. Hold it open just enough to let us out one at a time. Let's do it!'

It was a breeze: the latch didn't click as it lifted, the door swung back noiselessly. They ducked out into the porch, carefully closed the door behind them and breathed in the cool dark, punching one another's shoulders, almost hugging in delighted relief.

'Piece of cake!' John giggled.

'Dead easy!' agreed Zit Face. 'But if anybody'd tried anything on, I would've decked 'em.'

'Er...Ross?' the runt said. 'I don't remember this. We came in right off the street, didn't we?'

'Yeah – why?'

'The street's gone.'

John looked and swore.

The porch faced the high wall of an alley that was blocked at both ends. John stepped over to the wall and pressed his hands against it, as though he might push his way through.

'This wasn't here before!' he said hoarsely.

'There's a lot of stuff in Stanstowe that wasn't there before,' said the runt.

John forced himself to stay calm.

'Chill, lads,' he said. 'There has to be a way out. Doors don't lead nowhere, do they?'

They found the way out two nerve-shredding minutes later, a steep flight of steps with a metal handrail. Somehow, the steps managed to spiral round the wall, but John didn't stop to think how impossible the arrangement was.

'I'll go first,' he said. 'There could be someone at the top,' and he began to climb – and climb, and climb, until his breathing was laboured and his knees screamed for rest.

Out of condition, John thought. I ought to cut out the booze and fags, sign on at a gym and get in shape.

Then he heard the puffing and blowing of the teenagers behind him, and didn't feel so bad about himself.

'Long way up, isn't it?' gasped Zit Face.

'Save your breath!' John panted.

At last, the end of the steps and the top of the wall came into sight. John hauled himself over, Zit Face and the runt close behind him.

They were on the roof of the temple. A low parapet separated them from a dizzying drop, the dome was at their backs. Over to the right, a gargoyle hunkered on a plinth, a bigger than life-sized man-lizard with scaly wings.

'Something weird's going on!' the runt said unnecessarily.

'Great view though!' said Zit Face.

John was in no mood to appreciate the vista.

'Stuff the view!' he snapped. 'This is nuts! What the hell are we doing up here?'

'Maybe that bloke in the black leather coat hypnotised us,' said the runt. 'Maybe the street's really there, but we're not seeing it.'

'Yeah?' said John. 'Well if you'd like to be the first to try stepping over the edge, be my guest, mate.'

Something twitched beneath their feet.

Zit Face glanced down, and saw that the parapet was growing. New blocks appeared, squeezing the other blocks aside. The parapet bulged and contracted, as if it were breathing.

'It's alive!' Zit Face shouted. 'The temple's alive!'

The gargoyle stretched its arms and wings, yawned extravagantly and rasped its tongue over its muzzle. It clambered off the plinth, glared at the three who had intruded into its domain, and gave a low stone growl.

'Tell you what, lads,' said John. 'I reckon getting out of this place is going to be trickier than we thought.'

At eleven o' clock, the nine divided into two groups for the journey to Stanstowe Hill. Ollie and Scott joined Miss Morgan in her car. Dido, Cosmo, Philippa and Tom went with Mum and Dad.

It was a tight squeeze in the back seat. Cosmo spread herself on Dido's lap and purred as Dido stroked her. The temperature had risen, and the snow was melting into slushy pools. The car slid about until Dad turned on to Stanstowe Road, where the going was firmer. They passed many snow sculptures. Most had crumbled with the thaw, reduced to grey stumps like rotten teeth.

Doubts crowded in on Dido. In theory, she'd come of age as a Light Witch on her thirteenth birthday, but she didn't feel very grown-up.

How can I stop the Supreme Power of Shadow

Magic? she thought. I'm a teen! I ought to be dating, listening to boy bands, throwing wobblies if I don't get the right designer labels – not going one-to-one with a god!

Magic had shaped Dido's life, though she sometimes thought that 'warped' would be a more accurate description. It had set her apart from other children, and she hadn't made any close friends until she moved to Stanstowe and met Scott, Philippa and Ollie. She'd given magic most of her spare time, to the exclusion of other things that most girls of her age would consider normal.

And it's all been leading up to this, Dido thought. I've already sacrificed loads, what else have I got to give?

'Are you scared, Dido?' Philippa asked.

'Kind of,' said Dido. 'I think it's stage fright, but I've never been on stage, so I wouldn't know.'

'Stage fright?'

'I have to give my best performance ever. Trouble is, someone forgot to give me a script.'

The interior of the car suddenly went black.

'What happened to the street lights?' said Tom.

'There must have been a power cut,' Dad said.

Dido craned her neck to look through the

windscreen. There was nothing but darkness beyond the twin cones of the car's headlamps.

'This is like when I was little,' Mum said. 'I used to think that when I was in a car, it stayed still and the world moved under it.'

Dad consulted his watch.

'That might not be far off the truth,' he said. 'We should be going uphill by now.'

A lilac glimmer lightened the darkness. Rags of shadow whirled around the car and buffeted it from side to side.

Voices came out of the night. A baby wailed; a dog howled; a young child pleaded, 'Help me! Help me! Isn't there anyone who can help me?'

'Keep going, Dad!' Dido urged. 'Spelkor's trying to distract us.'

A spell surged out of her, the strongest and strangest spell that she'd ever cast, so strange that she couldn't tell if it came from Light or Shadow Magic. The spell had a rising tide in it. White-crested waves broke along the shore of a rocky bay, below a sky that was paling into dawn as the rim of the sun showed over the horizon. A flock of white birds flew over, their feathers showing soft pink and grey in the early light. Out in the bay a whale sounded, its spout slanting in the wind.

The tide washed away the spiralling shadows. The bay and the birds faded, leaving trees at the side of the road. The car was climbing Stanstowe Hill.

High above, Comet Bailey-Hooper shone yellow-white, as if a rip had been torn in the night and tomorrow was leaking through.

16
All the Fun of the Fair

Dad pulled in at the top of Stanstowe Hill.

'Everybody stay in the car until the others arrive,' he said. 'They shouldn't be long.'

Mum gazed at the Speaking Stones.

'This is a real letdown,' she said. 'I expected some sort of reception committee.'

'It's not midnight yet,' Dido pointed out. 'That's when the action starts.'

'Talking of action, where did that spell of yours come from?' Mum asked curiously.

'Inside.'

'What made you choose it?'

'I didn't. It chose me.'

Tom's face screwed up in bewilderment, and Philippa coughed nervously. She'd never been comfortable with Dido's magic – even though it had saved her neck more than once. Like Scott and Ollie,

Philippa made jokes about the fact that Dido was a witch, but Philippa's jokes masked her uneasiness.

Dido's eyes wandered to the circle. The first time she saw it – long before she knew anything about Spelkor – it had given her the creeps. Most ancient monuments were messages from the past that no one knew how to read – mysterious, but in a peaceful way. The Speaking Stones were anything but peaceful. They were sinister and restless, as though they had unfinished business to attend to. Tonight the circle seemed out of place, shards of grey darkness, lancing through the soil like jagged fangs.

The stones are hungry, Dido thought. They want to feed on the world.

Light shone into the car as Miss Morgan's car drew up behind. The nine gathered at the side of the road. Mum wrapped her arms around herself and shivered.

'You were always right about this place, Dido,' she said. 'It's evil.'

Dido raised her eyebrows.

'You used to tell me it was the most tranquil place in Stanstowe,' she said.

'I lied,' Mum admitted. 'I thought that if I could

make you get used to it, you wouldn't find it so threatening.'

Cosmo nattered.

'What was that?' said Mum.

'Er, she said it was a sound plan,' Dido said, leaving out the second part of Cosmo's comment, which was, 'Shame it didn't work.'

Tom scowled.

'You talk to your cat?' he said.

'Sure,' said Dido. 'Doesn't everybody?'

'You're all bonkers!' Tom declared. 'I'm on top of Stanstowe Hill in the middle of the night, with a bunch of crazies. This can't be happening.'

'A common reaction to magic,' said Dad. 'Most people can't explain it, so they refuse to accept that it's there.'

'I wish I could,' said Ollie.

'Mmm,' Philippa said, nodding in agreement.

Scott edged round the others to stand next to Dido.

'Hey,' he said, 'that sacrifice thing you talked about. You're going to be all right, aren't you?'

'I don't know,' said Dido.

'The Dark One won't hurt you or anything, will he? Because if he so much as lays a finger on you, I'll—'

'You wouldn't be able to do anything to him, Scott.'

'Can I at least give him a dirty look?'

This was so like the old Scott – cracking a bad joke to lift the mood a little – that Dido laughed. 'I've missed you, Scott,' she said. 'All that boy-girl stuff kind of got in the way of how things ought to be, didn't it?'

'I suppose.'

'D'you know what I'm going to do when all this is over?'

'What?'

'Go to the coffee bar in Springer's bookshop and eat giant chocolate-chip cookies until I'm sick.'

Scott pulled a face.

'While you're being sick, don't forget to clench your teeth to hold the big bits back,' he said.

The alarm on Dad's watch started to beep. He switched it off and said, 'It's midnight.'

The stones wavered like smoke in the wind. Their outlines grew misty enough to see the tail of the comet through them. Then the mist thickened, rolling and billowing. Shadowy shapes formed within it.

'My thumbs aren't itching!' Dido said softly. 'Why aren't my thumbs itching? Something must be blocking them.'

'You need your *thumbs* to tell you this is magic?' Cosmo said in Cat. 'I can work that one out, and I don't even have thumbs!'

The shapes became clearer as the mist dispersed.

Dido didn't know what she was looking at. She saw a violet mountain, a golden-topped tower, spinning lights.

'A *fairground?*' Dad gasped.

'I think it's intended as an enticement,' Mum said. 'It's like a mousetrap – you smell the cheese, you nibble the cheese and wham! The Dark One appears to have some quaint ideas about what appeals to teenagers nowadays.'

The Dark One had got it spot on as far as Tom was concerned. His eyes opened wide.

'Brilliant!' he said. 'A fairground! Magic!'

'Exactly,' said Dido.

'Can we go in?'

'We have to,' Dido said. 'We were invited, weren't we?'

As Dido approached the fairground, its details came more into focus. What she'd taken to be a mountain was a switchback railway, and the tower was a helter-skelter. The rest was a jumble of roofs, striped awnings and billboards – Hall of Mirrors, Ghost Train, Penny Arcade. A gusting breeze carried the mixed scents of frying onions and hot sugar, and snatches of barkers' banter.

'Step right up, folks!'

'Thrills, chills and spills!'

'Prizes for everybody! Bunty pulls the strings!'

Dido paused at the entrance, a wooden arch that supported the neon sign. Tom ran past her, shouting, 'I'm going on the waltzer!'

'No, Tom!' Philippa called. 'Come back!'

Tom ignored her.

Philippa looked helplessly at Dido. 'What if we lose him in the crowd?' she wailed.

'We are the crowd,' said Dido. 'Haven't you noticed? Apart from the people on the stalls, we're the only ones here.'

'But I can't leave him on his own! He's my brother – I'm responsible for him.' Philippa hurried through the arch.

'And I'm responsible for all of you,' Dido said.

Dad put his hand on Dido's shoulder.

'Let her go, Dido,' he said. 'Spelkor's not interested in her.'

'Huh?' said Dido. 'What about the nine?'

'Seven is a magic number too,' said Mum.

'The Seven Deadly Sins,' Miss Morgan said.

'Seven days of the week,' said Scott.

'The seven hawks of Ra,' Ollie said.

He smiled at Dido. Mum, Dad, Miss Morgan and Scott wore the same smile.

'Uh oh!' mewed Cosmo.

Dido's thumbs itched, and her instant reaction was to go into inseeing.

Her companions seemed to be on fire. Pale lilac flames licked around them, the flames turning into tongues and teeth and claws. A disembodied mouth on a long neck of fire struck at her. Dido stepped back, swerving to avoid a slashing pair of talons.

Mistake! she thought. My thumbs must have been telling me *not* to use inseeing.

She made a shielding spell from a sheet of plate glass and the steel door of a bank's vault. The shield dropped in front of her and Cosmo. Claws screeched against the glass, setting Dido's teeth on edge. The mouth stunned itself on the steel and withdrew.

Dido went on to the attack. She imagined a torrential downpour, shaped a sword from the rain and hacked at the Shadow spell. The blade of the sword boiled into steam. She raised a gale that bent the flames back in tatters, but didn't blow them out.

It was a stalemate. The Shadow spell couldn't touch Dido any more than she could touch it.

The fire died down. Dido gingerly lowered the shield.

Dad was still smiling, like nothing had happened. Only Dido and Cosmo were aware that Spelkor's magic was at work.

'We should grab the chance to enjoy ourselves,' Dad said. 'We've all been under a strain these last few days. Let's relax.'

'In the Tunnel of Love, perhaps?' Mum said, linking arms with Dad and guiding him under the arch.

'And I fancy a turn on the dodgem cars,' said Miss Morgan, skipping after them.

Dido didn't try to cast a spell to bring them back, knowing it would be useless.

'I don't see a conjuror anywhere,' said Scott. 'Maybe they'll give me a job.'

He put his hands into his trouser pockets and strolled off, whistling along with the brass band.

Ollie's smile expanded into a grin.

'There's a shooting gallery over there,' he said. 'My

second sight should come in handy for that. Don't worry, Dido, I'll be fine.'

'Sure, but what about me?' Dido demanded.

'You'll be fine,' said Ollie, turning away.

Cosmo rubbed against Dido's ankles and made a rude remark about Spelkor's parentage.

'Yeah, but he's clever too,' said Dido. 'I've been conned. Spelkor let the nine of us get together to raise my hopes, now he's enchanted the others and isolated me. He's the kind of guy who helps little kids to build sandcastles so he can enjoy the looks on their faces when he kicks the sandcastles over. He's a practical joker, and practical jokers are bullies.'

The realisation made Dido feel better, until she remembered that bullies always selected victims who were weak.

'Get a grip, kid!' yowled Cosmo.

'You're right, Coz.' Dido stared at the sign and said, 'You don't get shot of me that easily, Spelkor. Ready or not, here I come!'

And Dido and Cosmo entered the fairground.

17
The Place of Letting Go

Philippa caught up with Tom at the foot of the wooden steps that led up to the mounting platform of the waltzer. She grabbed him by the arm and swung him round.

'What d'you think you're doing, running off like that?' she demanded angrily. 'Mr Nesbit told us to stay together.'

'Then how come you're not with the others?' said Tom.

'Because I came after you.'

Tom laughed scornfully.

'Don't give me that!' he said. 'You just wanted an excuse to get away. You think they're cracked as well, don't you?'

'They're not cracked, they have different ideas from most people, that's all.'

'Different as in *totally insane*?'

'Now then – none of that!' said a voice.

Philippa and Tom looked up.

A young man was at the top of the steps. He was wolfishly handsome, with dark curly hair and thick eyebrows. His clothes were purple – dark purple denim jeans and cowboy boots, a shiny purple shirt with the sleeves rolled back to reveal a five-pointed star tattooed on his left forearm.

'We don't like any arguments here,' he said.

'What's it to you?' said Tom.

The young man shrugged.

'This is a fairground,' he said. 'Our job is to make people happy. They come with the weight of the world on their shoulders. We provide them with a little magic and excitement, and their cares melt away. This is a place where you let things go. Leave your squabbles outside. If you don't, all our efforts will be wasted.'

The young man's voice was chocolate-smooth, and persuasive.

He's right, thought Philippa. I was stupid to get so worked up about Tom. There's nothing to be afraid of here.

'Are you going to ride the waltzer?' said the young man.

'How much?' said Tom, fumbling in the pocket of his jacket.

'Money isn't necessary.'

'Huh? You mean it's free?'

'Nothing is free,' the young man said. 'You'll pay, but in a way you won't expect.'

'What kind of way?' Philippa said suspiciously.

The young man smiled.

'If you don't take the ride, you'll never know,' he said. 'All rides are about gains and losses. It's for you to decide whether the pleasure you gain is worth the loss.'

Philippa hesitated. She wasn't entirely certain that what the young man had said made sense. When she tried to recall his words, they looped back on themselves and turned into a tangle of nonsense – *loss and gain, goss and lain, sog and slain ...*

Tom said, 'I'm up for it! Come on, sis – unless you're going to go all girly on me and wave as I go round.'

Philippa followed him up the steps, determined that he shouldn't ride the waltzer on his own.

The young man showed them into their chair, snapped the safety bar into place, then crossed the platform and worked a lever.

As the chair began to move, Tom had a moment of clarity.

'Hang on, I don't get this!' he said. 'What's a funfair doing on top of Stanstowe Hill?'

Philippa didn't hear the question. She'd thought that she and Tom were the only ones on the waltzer, but there was a woman seated in the chair directly opposite. She wore a dove-grey raincoat, a magenta headscarf and dark glasses.

The waltzer picked up speed. The gentle pivoting of the chairs accelerated to a violent spin. They lifted up and hurtled towards one another. The woman came rapidly closer until, just as the chairs seemed about to crash together, they were pulled back.

Philippa's stomach heaved, and not only because of the ride.

'Tom!' she whispered urgently. 'It's Mum. That woman over there is Mum.'

'It can't be,' said Tom. 'Mum's dead.'

'I know, but it's her!'

The ride continued, bringing Philippa's mother within touching distance, and then snatching her away.

'Mum!' Philippa yelled.

Her face was streaked with tears.

*

The floats in the Tunnel of Love were shaped as swans. After Mum and Dad clambered aboard the leading swan, they were approached by the ride's operator, a sharp-featured young man with curly dark hair and purple clothes.

'Tickets, please,' the young man said.

Dad was about to say that he hadn't bought any, when he noticed that he was holding a pair of tickets in his left hand. Part of him was puzzled by how they'd got there, another part told him to sit back and relax.

Mum snuggled close. The Shadow spell that had enchanted her made her feel cosy and warm.

The young man took the tickets, tore them in half and returned the stubs to Dad.

'Enjoy yourselves,' said the young man. 'But it never did run smooth, you know.'

'What – the ride?' said Dad.

'No,' said the young man. 'The path of true love.'

The swan glided towards a pair of doors that were decorated with a sparkling purple heart. The heart split in two as the doors opened. Darkness engulfed the float.

'I can't see a thing!' Dad grumbled.

'Silly boy!' said Mum. 'You don't go into the Tunnel of Love to look at things.'

Music played – an old hit from the Eighties. Somewhere, a projector whirred. A shaft of light stabbed through the dark. A home-made movie leapt on to a screen. The movie had been shot on film, not video, and the colours were faded. It showed a young couple with elaborate hairstyles bathing a baby girl. The baby jiggled, and slapped her palms on the surface of the water, spraying the couple.

Dad said, 'Faye, it's us – me, you and Dido.'

'What?' said Mum. 'It can't be. How did—'

A commentary interrupted her. The commentator was a man with a richly resonant voice.

'You did not choose for your daughter to be the Giver, any more than you chose her gift,' the voice said. 'Those were matters decided by others, long before she or you were born. This ride will show what your lives might have been, without the blight of magic.'

The picture on the screen flicked. Dido was a tousle-haired toddler, hugging a doll that was almost the same size she was, laughing and chattering silently.

'She never played with dolls!' Dad exclaimed. 'She

used to hate them. She called them *the still people*.'

'You don't understand,' said Mum. 'That's Dido without magic. That's what she would have been like.'

The picture shifted to a birthday party. Dido blew out six candles on a cake. Children seated around a table clapped and cheered.

'She has friends!' Mum said. 'She has so many friends. See how popular she would have been when she was younger, if she hadn't been a witch? All those lonely years! All that—'

The rest of the sentence was lost in a sob.

Unaware that she was being manipulated by Shadow Magic, Alice Morgan was having a great time. The good-looking, curly-haired young man who ran the dodgems had flirted with her, and insisted on not charging her. It didn't seem strange that all the dodgems were painted exactly the same shade of purple, or that they were being driven by alternative versions of herself, Alices she'd one day dreamed of becoming.

Alice the model was as thin as a rail and had cheekbones like a greyhound's. She was wearing a chic and expensive little black number. Her face showed no enjoyment; she'd trained herself not to frown or smile, in order to avoid wrinkles. Alice the rock star was in a leather catsuit, swigging champagne straight from the bottle and steering her car all over the place, to the evident disapproval of Alice the academic, who wore a mortarboard and rimless glasses. Alice the mother shared her dodgem with two plump, gurgling infants. Alice the champion show-jumper had a riding hat on her head, and a huge silver cup beside her on the seat. Alice the astronaut slow-motion waved in zero gravity.

Alice laughed out loud. She could stay on the dodgems forever, meeting an endless number of other Alices.

Of course, she had to bump them all.

Scott didn't have to go far. Almost as soon as he was inside the fairground, he spotted the big sign with his name on it – or his stage name anyway – spelled out in purple lights:

VOODINI, MASTER OF ILLUSION

Below the sign was a stage kitted out with top-of-the-range conjuring props – a table covered with a black cloth, a large trunk and a glass tank filled with water for an escape routine, a coffin on stilts for sawing a lady in half, and any number of ropes, hoops, juggling balls and silk scarves.

A dark-haired young man was waiting at the bottom of a flight of wooden steps that gave access to the stage.

'Voodini!' the young man said. 'You made it!'

'You know who I am?' said Scott.

'Conjuring's a small world,' the young man said dismissively. 'The stage is all yours. Show us what you can do.'

A travelling spotlight followed Scott up the steps and on to the stage. Scott didn't remember changing, but all of a sudden he was dressed in a dinner suit and a purple velvet cloak. He stopped at the table. In its centre was a deck of cards with a purple tartan design printed on their backs. Scott split the deck, shuffled the cards and fanned them out in both hands.

I can do anything tonight, he thought. Every trick I try will come off – even the tricks I don't know how to do.

He dealt out the cards in rows, face up on the table. The lower-value cards were normal, but the faces on the court cards were the faces of people he knew. The Queen of Hearts was Dido. Philippa was the Queen of Diamonds. Ollie was the Jack of Spades, and the Jack of Clubs was Scott himself. Miss Morgan, Mr and Mrs Nesbit and Scott's parents were there too.

Intrigued, Scott moved the faces around, putting them in different combinations – Dido next to Ollie, then Philippa, then himself. He put his father next to Mrs Nesbit, his mum next to Mr Nesbit. There was an infinite variety of combinations.

All Scott had to do was to find the combination that was right.

Ollie lifted the rifle off the counter. It was surprisingly heavy, but well balanced. The barrel was black with a purple sheen. There was a mark on the wood of the stock, from the countless faces that had pressed against it.

'This is a real gun,' Ollie said.

'Certainly is,' said the young man behind the counter, running a hand over his dark curls. 'It's a Two-Two calibre. Belgian.'

Assuming this to be significant, Ollie did his best to look impressed.

'Shooting's a top way to forget your troubles,' the

young man continued. 'You have to concentrate on the target, find the right line and the right time. If you're going to get it perfect, you can't afford to think about anything else – and squeeze the trigger gently, don't yank at it. Are you ready?'

'I guess,' said Ollie.

He raised the rifle to his shoulder and sighted along the barrel. The targets were ping-pong balls, riding on the tops of water jets. Ollie made his selection, squinted, and the ping-pong ball became transparent. Inside was an image of himself and Philippa, standing outside Stanstowe Town Hall, holding hands. Ollie didn't know how he could see everything in so much detail when the ball was at the far end of the shooting gallery. He moved the rifle to another target. It showed the same scene, but Philippa was holding hands with Scott.

'Take it easy,' the young man coaxed. 'All your troubles, right? Bang – there goes one. Bang, bang, bang!'

Ollie held his breath and squeezed the trigger.

Dido and Cosmo wandered the fairground for a long time. Dido was deep in thought. Her Shadow Magic had been so wild and unpredictable that handling it had been like riding a bucking bronco, but at the entrance to the fairground, when she'd needed her Shadow Magic to hold the nine together, it had failed her.

Why was that? she wondered. Did Spelkor do it? Won't my Shadow Magic work against him, because it knows he's its master? Or was it an illusion, fooling me into thinking I couldn't use it?

'Hunk alert!' mewed Cosmo.

Dido came out of herself. She and Cosmo were in front of a tiny purple tent. A spectacularly handsome young man with dark curly hair was holding the flap of the tent open.

'Now here's a young lady with a lot on her mind,' he said slickly. 'Let it go. Step inside and consult Karnak, swami extraordinary. The past and present are one to him. He'll tear aside the veils that hide your future. What does fate have in store for you? Karnak knows.'

'That's it?' growled Cosmo. 'That was the big sell? I like him better when he keeps his mouth shut.'

'Wait, Coz,' Dido said. 'Ollie told me to look for what I need, and a fortune-teller is it.'

'It's a come on,' warned Cosmo. 'He's going to tell you a load of stuff about going on long journeys and meeting tall, dark, handsome strangers.'

But I *have* met a tall, dark, handsome stranger, thought Dido, gazing at the young man. 'Sure,' she said to him. 'Why not? Is it OK if I take my cat with me?'

'All are welcome,' said the young man. He held the flap open wider, and Dido and Cosmo ducked in.

The interior of the tent was far bigger than its outside. It was lit by oil lamps suspended from poles. Two lines of poles ran off into the distance. Another source of light cast a bright circle around a small round table. On top of the table was a crystal ball.

'A spirit mirror!' whispered Dido.

Someone in the shadows behind her said, 'I believe that the customary greeting on an occasion such as this is – "So, we meet at last." But you and I are beyond such clichés, are we not? Allow me simply to say, hello, Light Witch.'

'Hello, Spelkor,' said Dido, and turned around.

18
The Test

He was average – neither tall nor short, thin nor muscular, old nor young. The navy blue and purple pinstriped suit that he was wearing wouldn't have looked out of place on a businessman or a headmaster. He was almost bald; what hair he had left was steely grey. His features were strong: a hooked nose, a thin-lipped mouth, close-set eyes that slanted upwards at the corners.

'You don't look much like a god,' Dido said.

To her amazement, Spelkor burst out laughing. The laugh softened his face and brought a twinkle to his pale eyes.

'A god?' he chortled. 'It would appear that my enemies have exaggerated my abilities somewhat. I am no god.'

'But you're thousands of years old!'

Spelkor shook his head.

'I am the age I seem,' he said. 'My magic allows me to move freely through time, so I can exist both here and long ago, but I cannot make myself any younger. Eventually I shall grow older and die, like any other witch. Do you find my appearance unacceptable? I could arrange something more godlike, if you would prefer.'

Spelkor's suit whitened. The material moved, reweaving itself into a purple-trimmed toga. A circlet of laurel leaves rested on his brow.

'This guy *has* to be kidding!' Cosmo yowled.

Spelkor raised an eyebrow.

'Your familiar does not approve,' he said, as his toga reverted to a suit. 'All this human chatter must be tedious for her. Perhaps some feline company is called for.' He looked down. 'Kanno deeth, Valuminal!'

A tomcat emerged from under the table, an elegant lilac-point Siamese.

'This is my familiar, Valuminal,' said Spelkor. 'Your cat must have much that she wishes to discuss with him.'

'Nice eye candy!' Cosmo purred.

She and Valuminal brushed whiskers, made enquiring squeaking noises and then embarked on a conversation in Cat that was too rapid for Dido to follow.

'But I forget my manners,' said Spelkor. 'Can I offer you anything, Light Witch?'

He nodded at the table. It expanded and mirror-polished itself. Plates, cutlery and a silver candelabra rose up through it. Napkins bobbed to its surface like floating corks.

'No thanks,' said Dido. 'What have you done to the others?'

'Ah yes – the rest of the nine! They are otherwise engaged and going nowhere. Have no fears on their behalf, I have no intention of harming them...unless it becomes necessary.'

'And what would make it necessary?'

'A lack of co-operation on your part,' Spelkor said breezily. 'A display of stubbornness. Believe me, I have no desire for any unpleasantness. Contrary to the rumour spread by my opponents, I do not have a cruel nature, Light Witch.'

Dido was puzzled.

'Why d'you keep calling me *Light Witch?*' she asked.

Spelkor was taken aback.

'Because you are a Light Witch,' he said. 'Should

I call you by another name?'

'Light Witch will do fine,' said Dido, and thought, *He doesn't know about the Twilight Magic. He has limits. I must keep him talking and find out more.*

'Shall we be seated?' said Spelkor.

They sat facing each other across the table. Spelkor lifted a finger and the table settings disappeared.

'Would you think it rude of me if I took refreshment?' he said.

'Go ahead.'

Spelkor frowned.

'Let me see,' he murmured. 'It has been quite some time, but—'

There was a sound like the singing of a glass. A crystal goblet of red wine materialised in Spelkor's hand. He sniffed at the wine, swallowed a mouthful and sighed.

'St Emilion, 1928,' he said. 'An exceptional vintage.'

'All this is pretty impressive,' said Dido, turning on the flattery.

'All this?'

'The fairground, the weather, the chaos.'

Spelkor pursed his lips.

'Thank you for the compliment, but it represents the merest hint of what I can do,' he said. 'It affords the briefest glimpse of my power.'

'Yeah? I guess that would be the power you stole from the Goddess,' said Dido.

Spelkor's eyes gleamed purple with rage.

'I stole nothing, Light Witch!' he snapped. 'Your precious Goddess is the real thief. She took all the power of Light for herself and left the world helpless in the darkness.'

'Why would she do that?'

'Why?' Spelkor repeated with a hollow laugh. 'Because she is vain and greedy, and will not share her power with anyone. You did not know her then – her terrible beauty, the coldness of her scorn, her spiteful whims – but I suffered all. If I had not rescued Shadow Magic from her clutches, everything would have been lost. Even then she tricked me with her soft words, trapped me, kept me prisoner for four thousand years. Do you know what that means, Light Witch? Can you imagine what it is to be left a will, but no form to carry out that will?'

'Boring, huh?' said Dido.

'Suffering beyond endurance!' Spelkor cried, then

composed himself. 'And yet I endured it,' he added calmly.

Dido's mind whirled. Spelkor's version of the Goddess was nothing like the all-caring, all-forgiving mother figure that Dido had been taught about.

Is it true? she thought. Or is he twisting the facts to make himself look hard-done-by?

'I am much abused and misunderstood,' said Spelkor. 'I have been treated unjustly and betrayed by one who was precious to me. All I hope for now is that the balance will be set straight, and that what is rightfully mine will be returned to me.' His voice shrank to a whisper. 'I must apologise for imposing all this on you, Light Witch. It has been too long since I had someone to talk with. Of the many agonies I have been put through, loneliness is the worst. To lose others is to lose oneself, to doubt one's own existence.' His eyes were distant. 'One forgets so much.'

Dido felt a pang of sympathy. Like Spelkor, magic had made her lonely for a long time, and left her lost in darkness. In a strange way she admired this noble-looking man, with his wise, hurt eyes – especially now that she could see the aura that surrounded his head like a crown, its wavering gold light shot through with crimson streaks of regret.

I could learn a lot from him, Dido thought. He knows the answers to questions I haven't even thought of.

A violent hissing and the screech of a cat distracted her. Valuminal bolted down the avenue of lamps in a beige blur, wailing in frustration and defeat.

Cosmo vaulted on to the table, her fur puffed up, making her look twice her normal size. She fixed her eyes on Spelkor and growled, 'Don't listen to him, Dido – he's lying!'

Dido was shocked out of her delusion. Only a few hours before, Dad's life had been threatened by Shadow Magic, and there'd been nothing noble or wise about it. Spelkor wasn't abused or misunderstood, he was a master liar, a ruthless exploiter of people's weaknesses.

'You used a glamour spell on me!' Dido exclaimed.

The golden halo around Spelkor's head burst. He made a shrugging gesture.

'A pardonable subterfuge,' he said. 'A small deception often eases matters along.' He mock-bowed to Cosmo. 'Well done, familiar! I obviously underestimated your ability. You are fortunate to have such an astute companion, Light Witch. Though excellent in many respects, I regret to say that Valuminal lacks courage. My fault entirely. I have spoilt him with too much pampering. I recall that when he was a kitten, he would—'

'Let's lose the stroll down Memory Lane and cut to the chase, shall we?' Dido said abruptly. 'You're holding my parents and friends hostage. What d'you want?'

Spelkor's smile was dangerous.

'You know what I want, Light Witch,' he said.

'I do? Why don't you come out and say it so we can both be sure?'

Spelkor raised his eyes towards the roof of the tent.

'Can it really be that she does not know?' he said. 'Has a child been sent to perform the task of an adult, or is she a decoy, sent to distract me from the *real* Giver?' He looked at Dido. 'Is that it, Light Witch? I can sense your magic, but how deep does it go? How strong are you?'

Dido met his gaze and said, 'Why don't you try me and find out?'

Spelkor's face hardened.

'Very well,' he said, pushing back his chair and standing upright. 'I shall put your magic to the test, and if you fail, you will be cast into everlasting oblivion.'

The dark beyond the lamplight seethed. Shadows coursed into Spelkor and his shape changed. His skin peeled back until bone showed under his flesh, his suit became a billowing black robe. He was a skeleton, mounted on a rusted iron horse. The horse reared, whinnying shrilly, its metal joints clanking and clattering. It huffed steam and sparks from its nostrils.

Spelkor's teeth glinted in an ivory grin. He pointed a white finger at Dido and time came out of it, washing over her, its undertow plucking at her ankles.

Dido's body aged. Her knees and elbows stiffened, her spine arched under the weight of the years pressing down on it. She felt wrinkles crease her face as her hair whitened and cataracts dimmed her sight. Her fingers cramped into claws.

Dido's magic stirred. A spell surged through her, sending thick clouds of dust into the tent. The dust swirled like water around the plughole of a draining bath. Dido knew that she was looking at the black nothing of the forever that had existed in the cold deeps of space before time began. At the centre of the vortex a black ball condensed, then pulsed into pure light as the dust ignited into a minature star.

Time ran backwards. Dido was young again.

The iron horse disappeared and Spelkor reverted to his businessman form.

'You have passed the test, Light Witch,' he said. 'You are the true Giver and yours is the sacrifice. You are one, but we are many.'

Spelkor doubled, the second Spelkor sliding off him to stand at his side.

'We are many!' the two Spelkors shouted, and split into four, and eight, and sixteen, doubling with every echo of their voices.

'We are many!'

Spelkors seethed in a massive crowd. They filled the tent, packed the lamplit avenue for as far as Dido could see.

'What is the sacrifice?' roared the crowd. 'What is the sacrifice?'

Faces flashed through Dido's mind – Mum, Dad, Cosmo, Ollie, Scott, Philippa.

Is that the sacrifice? she thought. Do I have to give one of them up? How can I?

'Sacrifice!' bellowed the crowd. 'Sacrifice, sacrifice!'

Dido thought of the rest of the crone's riddle.

Where strength and weakness are the same,
There love is hate and loss is gain.

The answer came gradually. It was the dearest thing in her life, but it had also cursed her, giving her strength as a witch but weakness as a person. She had loved and hated it passionately. Now she was being asked to lose it and she couldn't tell what the gain would be.

'My magic!' she called out. 'I offer you my magic, Lord Spelkor!'

The legion of Spelkors condensed into one. His eyes gloated triumphantly.

'I accept your sacrifice, Light Witch,' he crowed. 'Your magic will be consumed by mine, and after you others will follow, until the whole race of Light Witches has perished.'

A spell shaped itself on the table. It had crab-legs, and wheels. Jointed metal arms jutted from its shell, arms that ended in coils of metal like corkscrews, blades, spikes with hooked points. The spell rolled and scuttled towards Dido.

She closed her eyes. Loss is gain! she told

herself. Loss is gain!

Something entered her skull and ran through her neck, torso and limbs, as cold and heavy as mercury. Pain flashed red, then white, as something was wrenched out of her.

Dido saw a jerky stream of memories – a pentagram, her parents' grimoire, Lilil, the winged horse that had once flown her to the centre of her magic, her first witch-light, the sleek black panther that was the spirit of her Shadow Magic. They fell away from her, shrinking to a minute speck that winked out.

Dido felt raw and empty. Warm tears coursed down her cheeks. Slowly, she opened her eyes.

Spelkor was over three metres tall, and growing by the second.

'This is what I have waited for!' he said. 'This is what I dreamed of in my dungeon. This—'

He broke off and looked down at himself. His forehead suddenly bulged, as though something were trying to push its way out of his head. Pulsing veins glowed red through the skin at his temples. His face twisted. His fingers swelled like inflating balloons. Beneath his suit, his body seemed to be boiling.

'This – is – not – Light – Magic!' he panted,

fighting for breath. 'What – have – you – done – child?'

Spelkor melted, his face trickling on to his chest, his empty clothes collapsing into a heap. Where he had stood, a ball of impossibly bright grey light wavered, then exploded silently, sending out a huge ripple of shadow that moved at incredible speed.

It struck Dido full force, and she went down, and down, and down.

19
Loss and Gain

John was ripped away from a place that shouldn't have been there, and thrust into a place he didn't recognise. He was standing in front of a glass wall that was engraved with two huge stars. Beyond the wall were signs, lights, windows and a motionless escalator. People crowded around him. They seemed puzzled, like they didn't know what they were doing there. Come to that, John didn't know what *he* was doing there.

Where am I? he thought.

Then he clocked the person next to him, a big guy in a black leather coat, and remembered. His old mate Bivco had turned up out of the blue. They'd gone out to celebrate the reunion, and celebrated a bit too hard. John had invited Bivco to crash in his bedsit, and on the way they'd stopped here, so that Bivco could take a shuftie at the Pentacle. The mall hadn't been built the last time that Bivco was in Stanstowe, and he seemed stunned by it.

'Impressive, eh, Biv?' John said.

Bivco jerked, startled.

'What's that?' he said.

'The Pentacle. Didn't have anything like this in our day, did we?'

'Too right!' said Bivco. 'Here, Johnno, where were we just now?'

'In the Tudor Arms. Before that we went to the Star, and before that it was...er...' John giggled drunkenly. 'Ah, who cares?' He hefted a six-pack that he hadn't been aware he was holding. 'Let's go back to my place and chew the rag some more. Hey, remember Sally Maidment?'

Bivco rolled his eyes and groaned.

'Who could forget Sally Maidment?' he said. 'She was the hottest babe in our year. What happened to her?'

'Married Dave Reynolds, didn't she?'

Bivco's jaw dropped.

'What, wimpy Dave Reynolds, the swot?' he said. 'Never!'

'Straight up,' said John. 'Come on, I'll tell you all about it.'

They walked off through the rapidly dispersing crowd.

Jack's world tilted like the deck of a ship at sea, spun slowly and deposited him in the Pentacle, halfway down the steps that led from a row of bars and cafes to the bank of the Thames. He felt so woozy that turning his head quickly didn't seem too clever an idea, so he took his bearings slowly. To his left was Ross, crumpled in a heap, snoring loudly. David was on his right, barely awake. His eyes had the fixed look of someone struggling to focus.

'I been asleep?' Jack demanded.

'Dunno,' said David, and hiccuped.

'How did we get here then?'

'Must've walked.'

Jack leaned forward.

'What the hell are we?' he said.

His foot dislodged an empty half-bottle of vodka that tumbled down the steps.

'Oh yeah!' Jack said, as much to himself as to David. 'That's right. Ross got the booze from that offie by the garage, didn't he?'

'Did he?' said David.

Jack consulted his watch.

'It can't be that late!' he exclaimed. 'My old man's going to do his nut!'

He tried to get up, but slumped back down as the world spun again.

'I'm well gone!' he said, feeling quite pleased with himself. 'Is that vodka all we had, or did Ross score something else?'

'I'm going to die,' David whimpered.

'No you're not. You're off your face, that's all.'

David burped and shivered.

'I saw things, Jack,' he said.

'When?'

'When what?'

'You said you saw things.'

David frowned.

'Did I?' he said. 'When?'

'Just now.'

'I didn't see anything just now. I'm not feeling so good, Jack.'

'You'll be all right.'

'No I won't. I'm going to—'

David threw up so spectacularly that it wasn't long before Jack joined him.

'I'm never going to do this again!' Jack gasped between heaves. 'I'm never going to do this again!'

*

The sound of traffic made Dido open her eyes. At first the bright sunshine blinded her, then her eyes adjusted themselves. She was on a street she didn't know, on the pavement outside a large Victorian house. Wherever she was, it wasn't Stanstowe. The houses were too grand, the elm trees lining the street were too massive, and the bustle of background noise was too loud.

London? Dido wondered. Manchester?

'Mind out!' said someone.

Dido stepped aside. A man in brown overalls walked past her, carrying a large cardboard box towards the back of a furniture removal lorry that was parked at the kerb. On the side of the lorry was painted:

HERMES & SON
WINGS ON OUR HEELS

The removal man was closely followed by a small, elderly woman with a shock of long, silvery-white hair. Despite her age, the woman was dressed in a blue silk baseball jacket, denim jeans and red trainers, but somehow the outfit didn't seem too young for her.

'Be careful with that box, it's fragile!' she warned the removal man.

'Right you are, missus!' he said cheerily.

The woman smiled at Dido.

'Moving is such a pain, isn't it?' she said.

She spoke as if she and Dido were old friends, but Dido couldn't recall having met her before.

'Excuse me,' Dido said. 'I wonder if you could help me? I'm not exactly sure where I am.'

The woman's smile broadened.

'That's not altogether surprising,' she said. 'In one sense, you aren't anywhere. Your actual physical self is still on Stanstowe Hill. The rest of you is here, with me.'

Alarm prickled at the back of Dido's neck.

'And you would be?' she said.

'I have many names,' said the woman. 'You and your parents usually call me the Goddess.'

Dido giggled nervously.

'But you're a little old lady!' she said.

'Yes, I am *here*. I chose this location and this form to be less intimidating. I thought we should talk. You must have a lot of questions for me.'

'I certainly do!' said Dido. 'Starting with what happened to Spelkor?'

'Lord Spelkor made a mistake,' the woman said. 'He thought he was taking your Light Magic from you, but you became a Twilight witch at your Covening. Your Twilight Magic was too pure for him. It annulled his power.'

'So you used me as a trap?' Dido asked indignantly.

'I didn't use you for anything, Dido,' said the woman. 'It was all your doing. You tempted Lord Spelkor into overreaching himself, and he couldn't resist. He wanted to corrupt Light Magic, but your Twilight Magic overwhelmed him.'

Dido shook her head as she tried to take everything in.

'Is Spelkor dead?' she said.

'His spirit has been banished into the Long Ago, where he can do no harm. His time is over.'

The consequences of what she'd done began to seep into Dido's mind.

'If Spelkor's out of the way, there can't be any Shadow Magic, can there?' she said.

'No, there cannot.'

The removal man walked by.

'Last box coming up,' he said.

'Good,' said the woman.

'Hang on!' Dido said. 'Where are you going?'

'Into the Long Ago with Lord Spelkor,' said the woman. 'My time is also over. Light Magic must pass away with me. From now on, there will only be Twilight Magic, as it was at the beginning.'

'Excellent!' said Dido, rubbing her hands in glee. 'That means I'm a top witch, doesn't it? I'll be able to do amazing stuff.'

'No, Dido,' the woman said sadly. 'Your sacrifice was real. You have no magic left, though you will be able to advise others on how to use theirs. Shadowmasters have lost their powers, and all Light Witches must learn how to be Twilight Witches. Their magic will not be the same as before, and they need to be taught how to use it. You must be a guide, not a traveller.'

Dido's disappointment was crushing.

'Oh!' she said. 'I thought I could go back to being a Light Witch.'

'That's impossible. Your magic wouldn't have worked if you hadn't offered it up willingly. But you will be rewarded.'

'How?'

'With the gift of yourself,' said the woman. 'Magic has been a burden to you, as well as a blessing. Now you are free.'

'To do what?'

'Live,' the woman said. 'Only the nine will remember the Time of the Stars. A forgetting has been placed on all the others who were touched by it. For them, it will be as though nothing happened.'

'But—'

The woman placed her hand on Dido's arm.

'I have to go, and so do you,' she said. 'Your family and friends are searching for you. You should not keep them waiting.'

The woman and the street faded away, leaving behind the Speaking Stones and the lights of Stanstowe at the foot of the hill. The funfair and the snow were gone. The circle felt empty and at peace.

Or is that me? Dido thought. Maybe that's not peace, maybe it's boredom.

She attempted to insee, but the familiar side step into magic didn't happen. It felt as if she'd been locked out of a garden where she used to play. The drab ordinariness of everything closed in around her.

Then Dido looked up and saw the comet, the cold streak of white light in the sky. For the first time, she noticed how beautiful it was, and the beauty made a quietness inside her.

Voices broke into her silence.

Mum shouted, 'Dido? Where are you?'

'I'm here!' Dido called back, and it was true. She was in a definite place at a definite time. Magic wasn't going to whisk her off and make demands on her; the future was hers.

There was a massive eight-way hug with Cosmo on the ground in the middle of it. After the hug, everyone talked at once.

'Are you all right? Your mother and I were—'

'We tried to insee you, but—'

'I did this trick with cards, and it was really—'

'So it was like really saying goodbye to Mum, and—'

'I never thought a shooting gallery would get me sorted out. You see—'

'And now I know that the best me I can be is who I am, because—'

'Hey, Dido, where did the fairground go?'

'OK, OK!' said Dido. 'I've got a lot of explaining to do, but can I do it later, please? I'm knackered.'

Cosmo curled around Dido's feet, reeling off a intricate mixture of mews, trills and purrs.

'I can't understand you, Coz,' Dido said miserably. 'I don't know what you're telling me!' And she burst into tears.

Epilogue
Special

Stanstowe behaved like somebody with a terminally bad hangover, dragging itself into reluctant wakefulness after a long night of feverish dreams. People paused in the middle of conversations, as if they were on the edge of remembering something important, but it always slipped away. It took a few days for the town to settle back into its routine. A team of meteorologists, despatched from Oxford University to investigate the freak weather conditions, asked plenty of questions but left more puzzled than when they arrived, and nicknamed Stanstowe 'Zombieville' because no one recalled noticing anything unusual.

Puzzlement reigned in the Nesbit household too, and routine proved more difficult to establish. Dido and Cosmo managed to communicate – it wasn't hard for Cosmo to make herself understood, especially when she was hungry – but without the uncanny clarity they'd once had, though they remained close, and Cosmo was still more Dido's cat than her parents'.

Mum and Dad were the real problem. They knew next to nothing about Twilight Magic, and despite patient tutoring from Dido, their first attempts to use it were clumsy to the point of disastrous. After Mum blew all the windows out of the sanctuary with a misjudged shielding spell, Dido took her aside and gave her a good talking to.

'You mustn't rush at it,' Dido chided. 'Twilight Magic's like a big puppy. You have to work with it, but if you're not firm right at the start, it'll get out of hand.'

'I can't get the hang of it,' Mum grumbled. 'I don't know where it's coming from.'

'From inside you, of course,' said Dido. 'That's where all magic comes from. Everybody has some kind of magic, but not everybody understands the best way to handle it.'

'That's true for you too,' said Mum.

Dido sighed.

'I wish!' she said. 'But I have to face facts, all my powers have gone.'

'Not all,' said Mum.

And though Dido asked her what she meant, Mum would only smile.

Dido hated it when that happened.

On the Saturday before Easter Sunday, Dido went into town in the afternoon to meet Scott, Philippa and Ollie outside the Town Hall, but when she got there, only Scott was waiting.

'Am I late or are you early?' she said.

'Neither,' said Scott. 'We're both on time.'

'So where are Philippa and Ollie?'

Scott shrugged.

'Who knows?' he said. 'But wherever it is, my guess is that they're there together.'

'Together as in ...?'

'I think so.'

Dido waited for a twinge of jealousy that didn't come.

'Well, well, well!' she said. 'I wonder if things will work out for them.'

'Excuse me?' snorted Scott. 'We're teenagers. We're not supposed to have things work out for us. If they did, we wouldn't have heartache and stuff. I'd wear something shrink-proof if I were you.'

'How come?'

'Because something tells me they're both going to use your shoulder to cry on.'

'Oh, super!' Dido growled.

Dido and Scott strolled through town, and wound up at the coffee bar in Springer's bookshop, which was where they usually went. Dido looked out through the window at the teeming Saturday shoppers in the Pentacle, thinking how different things would have been if she hadn't defeated Spelkor, and feeling a bit miffed that no one there would ever give her any credit for it.

'Dido?' Scott said cautiously. 'I haven't had a chance to ask you before, but what's it like not having magic?'

It was a question Dido hadn't dared to ask herself, and it took her a while to reply.

'Different,' she said finally. 'I'm more in control of myself now. I can't fall back on magic all the time, so I have to use my brain to solve problems. I make my own decisions, and it's a relief not to have to save the world. I can be myself, but sometimes I miss the way that magic used to make me feel that I was someone special.'

Scott boggled.

'Huh?' he said. 'Your magic had nothing to do with it. You *are* special, Dido. As a matter of fact, you're about the most special person I've ever met.'

'Get outta here!' Dido said, laughing.

But there was a warm glow inside her. Almost as soon as she'd discovered her magical powers, a part of her had longed to be free of them so that she could be normal.

And now that I am, I'm going to give it my best shot! she promised herself.

Other Red Apples to get your teeth into.

Chris d'Lacey

David soon discovers the dragons when he moves in with Liz and Lucy. The pottery models fill up every spare space in the house!

Only when David is given his own special dragon does he begin to unlock their mysterious secrets and to discover the fire within.

Pat Moon

Loads of secret stuff about BOYS, worry bugs, babies, enemies, etcetera, etcetera. Snoopers will be savaged by Twinkle (warrior-princess guinea pig).

Do Not Read This Book was shortlisted for the Sheffield Book Award

Michael Lawrence

Something's after Jiggy McCue! Something big and angry and invisible. Something which hisses and flaps and stabs his bum and generally tries to make his life a misery.
Where did it come from?
Jiggy calls in The Three Musketeers and they set out to send the poltergoose back where it belongs.

Shortlisted for the Blue Peter Book Award

Hilarious.
Times Educational Supplement

Wacky and streetwise.
The Bookseller

More Orchard Red Apples

The Fire Within	Chris d'Lacey	1 84121 533 3
The Salt Pirates of Skegness	Chris d'Lacey	1 84121 539 2
The Poltergoose	Michael Lawrence	1 86039 836 7
The Killer Underpants	Michael Lawrence	1 84121 713 1
The Toilet of Doom	Michael Lawrence	1 84121 752 2
Maggot Pie	Michael Lawrence	1 84121 756 5
Do Not Read This Book	Pat Moon	1 84121 435 3
Do Not Read Any Further	Pat Moon	1 84121 456 6
How to Eat Fried Worms	Thomas Rockwell	1 84362 206 8
How to Get Fabulously Rich	Thomas Rockwell	1 84362 207 6
How to Fight a Girl	Thomas Rockwell	1 84362 208 4

All books priced at £4.99